Y0-BZS-351

Dear Reader,

What is it about a bad boy that sends an otherwise intelligent woman into a brainless, downward spiral? So maybe he's hot. Big deal, right? As thinking creatures, we can control our hormonal urges.

Well...maybe in our right minds we can. And frankly, it's easier to see the problem when it's someone else's—especially if she falls for the same guy, over and over. I've seen it happen—made me want to bang my head against the wall. It's as though she's addicted to the guy! If only she would open her eyes and see the real world....

That's where a loyal, street-smart girl pal comes into play. One like my character Cassie. She'll play psychiatrist, bully, pimp, and all-around punching bag to rescue her best friend from an on-again off-again boyfriend. Now, there's friendship for you.

I consider Cassie a tribute to some savvy girlfriends of my own—who always gave me a swift kick when I needed it most (not that I necessarily appreciated it at the time, mind you<g>).

Wishing you love, laughter and loyal pals,

*Natalie Stenzel*

P.S. I love to hear from readers! Drop by my Web site at www.NatalieStenzel.com.

# How does a girl get over her fear of flying?

"Nick, that door rattled when you closed it. You know that? You're taking us up into the sky with a rattling door. If that thing opened, we'd both get sucked out of the plane and plunge to horrible deaths. Right?"

He grinned at Cassie. "I suppose it could happen. *Whoosh*, and one hell of a ride down."

"I'm serious. I've seen sturdier doors attached to a fence post."

He sighed. "Relax, Cassie. First of all, a plane this size doesn't fly high enough that the cockpit needs to be pressurized, so there would be no 'whoosh' effect if—against all odds—the door flew open. It'd get a little windy in here, but we just might escape death by whoosh. And second, yes, the door is light. It's light so we can fly. But it won't open midflight and we're not going to die."

"You're sure?"

He raised his eyebrows.

She made a face. "At least you're honest. Fine. What do I do first?"

"Get in. We always fly inside the plane. It's safer that way."

What a girl wouldn't do to get a third date....

# Pop-Up Dating
## Natalie Stenzel

# HARLEQUIN®

TORONTO • NEW YORK • LONDON
AMSTERDAM • PARIS • SYDNEY • HAMBURG
STOCKHOLM • ATHENS • TOKYO • MILAN • MADRID
PRAGUE • WARSAW • BUDAPEST • AUCKLAND

ISBN 0-373-44186-X

POP-UP DATING

Copyright © 2004 by Natale Stenzel.

## ABOUT THE AUTHOR

Natalie Stenzel was a girl who just couldn't keep her nose out of (gasp!) a romance novel. Still, she denied her dreamy inclinations long enough to earn respectable degrees in English literature and magazine journalism from the University of Missouri-Columbia. She even flirted with business writing and freelancing for a while, considered going back to school for another respectable degree...only to return to her one true love: romance. Born and raised in St. Louis, Missouri, Natalie now resides in lovely Virginia with her husband and two children, happy to live a dream (or several) come true.

## Books by Natalie Stenzel

HARLEQUIN FLIPSIDE
4—FORGET PRINCE CHARMING

Don't miss any of our special offers. Write to us at the following address for information on our newest releases.

Harlequin Reader Service
U.S.: 3010 Walden Ave., P.O. Box 1325, Buffalo, NY 14269
Canadian: P.O. Box 609, Fort Erie, Ont. L2A 5X3

To Wanda Ottewell, editor extraordinaire,
for tireless brainstorming;
for understanding my mindless ramblings;
and for having the temerity to love
this outrageous story as much as I do.
Thank you.

# Step 1

*The Intervention*
*We admit to our girlfriends that our love lives*
*have become unmanageable.*

IT WAS JUST ONE OF THOSE modern-day truisms. Rain only fell on weekends or umbrella-less weekdays; the monthly curse always arrived on Friday or Saturday; and Robyn always forgave her boyfriend no matter how badly he behaved. Some things in a girl's life just remained constant and Cassandra Smythe listed these three as basic no-brainers.

But here she was, in her St. Louis apartment on a sunny Saturday afternoon, curse-free—though soon due—and witnessing the impossible. Her best friend, Robyn Wesley, was pissed, determined and—*finally*, praise God—ready to swear off her male addiction.

"I mean it this time, Cassie. I'm never taking him back. I've put up with a lot from Alex, but not this."

"You're serious."

"As a heart attack."

Cassie stared at her friend. Maybe she should have realized something like this would be the last straw. After all, in the three years Robyn had dated him, Cassie had watched, helplessly, as Alex proved himself an egocentric bastard in every clichéd manner possible. He hit on other women, took Robyn completely for granted and generally belittled or dismissed everything Robyn considered important in life. He rarely, in Cassie's opinion, even acknowledged Robyn's existence unless he needed money. And he frequently needed money.

But sainted, masochistic Robyn had borne up to every humiliating instance of it. Sure, she'd taken the occasional "break" from the relationship, but never, not until just five minutes ago, had Robyn dared to suggest to Cassie that she would actually dump the guy. And it had taken *this*?

"I still can't believe it." Robyn shook her head. "He actually called my work *commercial schlock*." She met Cassie's eyes. "Can you believe it? Just because I like to earn a paycheck with my artwork rather than starve in the streets."

"Totally mind-boggling." Cassie murmured it with feeling. She felt alarmingly like the straight man in a comedy skit, waiting for the punch line and yet hoping it wouldn't arrive.

"Exactly. Art comes in many forms and it's so intolerant of him to criticize just because the medium's less than traditional." She gave Cassie a fierce look. "But I don't care what he thinks. About me or my work. I'm *good* at what I do."

Shrugging off a guilty sense of irony, Cassie slid an arm around her friend's shoulders and squeezed. "Damn right you're good at it. You're not just an artist—you're an artist with an eye toward the future. A digital artist. A smart woman who knows the value of a cutting-edge medium for her talent. Displaying your work on Web sites like the ones I design will draw attention from surfers all over the world."

Robyn looked the tiniest bit hopeful. "You're sure?"

"Positive. Alex is just jealous because his own work isn't selling well. And you can't exactly translate sculpture into digital form." Cassie shrugged. "See? Professional jealousy. It's no wonder he was so rotten to you." *Oh, damn.* She hadn't meant to offer up a potential excuse for the parasite....

"Well, he can go pamper his own delicate little ego. I'm not crawling back to him this time."

*Thank God. A healthy dose of bravado...but which, if not bolstered, could shortly recede—* Cassie scrambled to reinforce. "You bet you're not. Even if I have to sit on you this time, you are *not* going back to that guy. He's no good for you."

Robyn gave her a vulnerable look. "So you think I did the right thing?"

Cassie bit back every word she wanted to say, contenting herself with a firm, "*Absolutely.*"

"Okay. So, okay, then." Robyn gazed around herself doubtfully, as though not sure where to go next. Not that their options were limitless.

As widely coveted as Cassie knew her apartment to be, with its lofty ceiling, decorative molding and hardwood floors, it was also modest in size. Her income was such that the furnishings were spare, as well. Not counting office furniture, Robyn basically had a choice of overstuffed couch, ancient wooden rocker or one of two ladder-back kitchen chairs.

Realizing all this decisiveness had temporarily para-lyzed her friend in thought and in movement, Cassie gently steered her toward the couch. Cassie swore she'd be supportive during this breakup, even if it killed her—and it might, if biting a hole through her tongue proved fatal.

Not that Robyn was a complete idiot. It was just that, like most addicts, she had a massive blind spot where her particular weakness—Alex—was concerned. Cassie could relate. She'd had a few blind spots herself.

Her ex-fiancé, for example.

Right out of college, Cassie had come *this* close to marrying a man she didn't love. At least Brad had worked up the nerve to suggest they call it off, even if it had been at the last minute. Her mother still hadn't completely forgiven Cassie for the expenses they'd had to write off, though Cassie had done her best to pay her back.

Even worse than the money and the humiliation, Cassie had had to deal with her mom's head-shaking and I-told-you-so's. She had always been convinced that Cassie—and every other intelligent female, for that matter—was better off without a man to clutter up her life. From beginning to end, according to her mother's logic, a man was always free to leave, while the woman was stuck first with the pregnancy and then with these funky maternal hormones that tied her to her kids no matter what. Lucky for Cassie, her mom had possessed more than her share of those lovely, funky maternal hormones. Cassie had always been able to count on her.

Soon after Cassie's graduation, however, her mom

had moved to California, leaving a big void in Cassie's life, though they still maintained frequent contact. In many ways, Robyn had stepped into that void. She was like family now. The eccentric artist second-cousin or something. Unfailingly lovable, but at this rate, destined for the funny farm. *Be nice, Cassie.*

Forcing her focus to the here and now, Cassie watched, pityingly, as Robyn carefully seated herself next to Cassie on the edge of a cushion. Then Robyn glanced around blindly, half stood, then carefully sat again, her hands gripping each other as if for comfort.

Cassie's heart twisted. "Oh, honey. You're going to be okay. I promise. I know you've invested a lot in this guy, but I swear we'll get you through it. Only good things will come out of this. You'll see."

Robyn gave her a doubtful look, but relaxed a little into the cushions. "I don't know. I'm not as strong as you are, Cassie." She shrugged a shoulder. "You'd never have put up with half the stuff I did. Oh, no. You'd have kicked him out...oh, God, *years* ago." Robyn stiffened, eyes widening in horror. "It's been years, Cassie. *Years.*" *And roll "Weakening For Alex" tape number three...*

"I know, I *know.* But—"

"That's a commitment, you know." Robyn shifted uneasily and crossed her legs. "Alex and I have been together for three years. That's a long time."

Too long. Cassie was aging quickly, thanks to this twisted relationship. "No, Robyn. *You've* been committed to *him* a long time. Alex..." Cassie shook her head, unwilling to take it further. Not nice to kick a girlfriend when she was down and any extrapolation, no matter how factual, would only hurt Robyn more. Oh, but if this guy cared at all about Robyn, he had a moronic way of showing it. Slow torture was too good for the jerk.

"He cared about me, Cass. He did. I'd swear he still does. Some guys just have a harder time with it than others, you know?" Robyn tugged at a chin-length dark curl. "Maybe I just gave up on him too soon. He has abandonment issues, you know. And I just abandoned him, so—"

Alarms went off in Cassie's head. *Ready to roll final tape, final scene, same old loop: weak, obsessed female crawls back to slimy boyfriend and*— "Oh, no. No, you don't." Cassie launched off the couch, pulling Robyn up with her. She turned so they faced each other. "To hell with Alex's abandonment issues. I'm abandoned, you're abandoned, *everyone's* been abandoned by someone or some thing."

Cassie, frankly, had no patience for people who blamed everything on their parents or a warped childhood. At a certain point it was just time for everyone to grow up and take responsibility for his or her own life. Live in the present, not the past. Besides, Cassie's mom had more than made up for whatever Cassie had lacked in her young life. It couldn't have been easy for her and Cassie admired her for it and looked up to her in many ways.

Still, despite all evidence to the contrary—primarily being that Cassie had never even met her own father, loser that her mother claimed he was—Cassie still wasn't convinced that she was intended to live her life alone.

Sure, her life was complete as it was. She had a challenging job that she loved, an apartment that felt like home and friends close enough to be considered family. That was a lot. And she was content to keep it that way indefinitely. After all, a man could only complicate a simple, gratifying lifestyle.

So Cassie figured any guy worth keeping had darn well better be the one she'd love for a lifetime and who felt the same way about her. That was one important lesson she'd taken from all of her mother's admittedly cynical lectures. Cassie refused to settle or to change her life for anything less than a man who could rock her world in a most wonderful way *for all time.*

It sounded impossible. Foolishly idealistic. But, like Robyn, Cassie wanted to believe that man was really out there, waiting just for her. The perfect man and the perfect love. She didn't exactly require him at this point in her life, but the shy, neglected romantic in her wanted to believe in the thrill of the fairy tale. The right man—and only the right man—could potentially add a whole new dimension to a girl's life. The tricky part was finding and identifying this paragon of a guy.

Since Cassie lacked any practical experience with long-term relationships or near role models in this arena, she'd long ago decided her only option was to trust that fate would lead her to her man. Assuming, of course, that she didn't let herself get tripped up by her own fickle wonderings and leanings.

In hindsight, Cassie could see that her engagement to

Brad had resulted from a huge vacuum of common sense and, quite possibly, haste and cowardice. Because, oh, boy, Brad might have been a walking blind spot for her, but he hadn't been nearly as threatening to her peace of mind as her infatuation preceding him.

Nick Ranger.

Wow. Forget mere blind spots. When Nick was around, Cassie had found herself deaf, dumb and blind to everything in the world but him. Luckily she'd had enough self-preservation to run in the other direction—even if it had led straight into Brad's arms and the wedding that didn't happen.

A smart woman would have known better and simply seen Brad for the fling he should have been. A man to help her shake off the unforgettable guy preceding him. What a mess that had been. All of it.

So, given that huge display of foolishness, who was *she* to criticize Robyn?

She could and would, however, help Robyn find her way through her own mess. Perhaps, along the way, she could help Robyn bypass some all-too-familiar mistakes. Now there was an idea. Maybe Robyn could profit from Cassie's own obsessive past.

"Listen, Robyn, I know you have doubts and I suppose that's only natural. But I am *not* letting you backslide because of them. Not now that you've made this kind of progress. I'm so proud of you for standing up for yourself. You're a talented, beautiful woman and *he never deserved you.* You were right to break up with him."

"But...what if he's the *one?* What if he's the one and

only guy who could show me fireworks and passion and...oh, *you* know." Robyn's eyes were pleading. "What if it's *him* and I'm giving him up?"

"It's *not* him. It couldn't be." Ignoring a tickle of uneasiness in her belly—that hand-of-fate feeling Robyn described that she wondered about too often herself—Cassie spoke as practically and matter-of-factly as she could manage. "Alex has done every rotten thing he could think of to shove you away. Does that sound like a one-and-only to you? Open your eyes, Robyn. See what everyone else can see. Any guy in his right mind would *grovel* for a chance with you."

Robyn considered her doubtfully. "You think so?"

"I know so. And we're going to go out and prove it."

"Oh, I don't think I'm ready for anything like that, Cass. I'm mad at Alex, but I still love the jerk."

Cassie winced at the familiar prelude. Oh, good Lord, but she couldn't do it again. Couldn't listen to the blissfully blind catalog of the wonders of loving Alex. Even *Cassie's* sense of the ridiculous—although admittedly overdeveloped—had some built-in limits.

Cassie spoke up quickly, forcefully. "That's just habit. You know it's just habit. You've been addicted to this guy for so long that being in love with him's just what you're used to. We can work on that. I know we can. We'll just...just—" Cassie glanced around wildly before hitting on a desperate solution. "We'll find someone to practice on."

"Practice on?"

"Well, yeah. Sort of." Robyn needed shock therapy, not just practice, but that wasn't the most diplomatic way of phrasing matters. Cassie impatiently shoved her hair behind a shoulder. "I was thinking more along the lines of…a temporary situation. To help you ease your way into a permanent one." *Transition. Yes. Good call, Cass.*

"Temporary? I'm not sure…you sound so business-like about it, like it's an easy thing to do, but I have no idea how to…" Robyn's eyes widened. "You can't mean like…like a male prostitute? A *gigolo?*" Robyn squeaked out what was, when coupled with herself, a near obscenity. "Oh, no. No way."

"No, not a *prostitute,* you dork. As though you'd need to *pay* for it." Cassie rolled her eyes.

"Well, then, how…?"

"We simply…advertise to the world of single men that you are available. Sort of like those annoying pop-up ads on the Internet. Sure, you close out of each and every one of them, but they do succeed in getting their message across, just through repetition." *Ooh. That was good, too. Metaphorical, powerful, convincing…*

"*Annoying?*"

*Oops.* "So the analogy only goes so far." Faking breezy confidence, Cassie waved off the details as unimportant. "Look, the point is, it shouldn't be too hard. You make yourself available and an interesting guy is sure to happen along. Just understand that I'm talking about a temporary…diversion. Someone to play with and make you feel good about yourself until you're ready to move on. It'll keep you from getting lonely and going right back to Alex."

"Oh, but I wouldn't…"

"You would."

Robyn sighed. "Well, *maybe* I would."

Cassie nodded. Admitting to a problem was always the first step. She knew that from experience. And, given a little help and diversion from temporary man, maybe Cassie could prevent Robyn from falling off the wagon into Alex's dubious care...or into the arms of her next blind spot. Maybe, with a little luck and cooperation, Cassie could keep Robyn from making a mistake like Brad. *Yes.* Once she got the transitional fling out of the way, Robyn could be happy, whole and aware when Mr. Right finally happened along.

"Okay. So here's what we're going to do. Tonight Becky's having her annual Saint Louis University alumni party. We've been invited and we're going."

"But you hate those parties."

Cassie laid a hand over her heart and assumed a saintly demeanor. "Consider it just one of the many sacrifices we make for our friends."

Robyn teared up again. "You're the absolute best, Cassie."

"I know. But I'm not going with you if you're going to leak all night. You're not, are you?"

Robyn wiped her eyes and straightened. "No. I'm done." She frowned, and Cassie could almost hear the words "commercial schlock" echoing in Robyn's mind. "He's not worth crying over. And I have a life to lead."

"Remember that." Cassie gave her an even but not unkind look and spoke in a similar tone. "So we're going to this stupid party tonight and you and I are going to check out the guys. You know Becky's a man magnet, so there's bound to be a decent male turnout at this thing. Who knows? Maybe I'll find a guy, too." She smiled gamely through her teeth.

"*Man magnet?* That's not what you usually call her." The voice might sound fragile still, but the gibe was all Robyn.

Cassie could have kissed her, she was so relieved. Instead, she just raised her brows, deliberately encouraging Robyn's attempt at lightheartedness. "Now, what kind of person would I be if I trashed the girl just before showing up at her party?"

Robyn smirked and Cassie felt downright cheerful. "A different *kind* of hypocrite?"

Cassie laughed.

Robyn's smile faded. "So you really think this will work? I should find a guy and just...have a fling with him?"

"I really, really do." Cassie tried to infuse every word with wise assurance. "It would break your bad habit and introduce you to new possibilities. You just have to remember that we're *not* looking for marriage material right now."

Robyn winced and spoke low. "Not that I've ever had it."

Cassie squeezed her shoulder. "One step at a time. First we get you over the addiction. *Then* we find you true love. So. Let's beautify and then go hunt up your temporary man."

# Step 2

*The Party Trawl*
*We come to believe in the wiles of a girlfriend with*
*more romance savvy than ourselves.*

"CAS-SAN-DRA! How *super* that you could make it!"
Becky sparkled and bubbled away as Cassie suppressed a wince. It was hard to take the woman seriously when everything she said could be punctuated
with exclamation points. Becky was only two years
younger than Robyn and Cassie, but she had the dis-
position and curvy body of a cliquish high-school
cheerleader.

"Becky. How are you? You look great." Cassie smiled
as the woman hugged her and then stepped back for a
quick appraisal.

"You look wonderful! And I heard you're making
just *oodles* of money with your new Web design business!"

Cassie blinked. *Oodles? Of money?* Maybe in Cassie's
wildest, most cherished dreams, perhaps. Obviously
someone had been spinning lovely fantasies on Cassie's
behalf. She peeked over her shoulder and encountered
Robyn's carefully innocent face. Ah. The fantasizer.
How could you not love her?

Touched, she cast a grateful look at Robyn and murmured to Becky, "Well, I'm not sure I'd call it oodles, but business is decent."

Sure, Robyn struggled with a really twisted case of co-dependence when it came to her love life. As a friend, however, she was a complete rock—and, given the smug little smile on Robyn's face, she'd obviously been bragging on Cassie behind her back. Probably at the gym, Cassie speculated, and probably, knowing Becky, not without provocation. If Becky dared to imply anything against Cassie, Robyn would sling verbal bricks on Cassie's behalf.

"Oh, that's just so...so *interesting*." Becky's fluttering lashes conveyed questionable sincerity. "James—he's my husband, you know—" Everyone knew. Becky wouldn't let them forget "—was telling me how even *his* business relies more and more on Internet commerce. It's a good thing he found an absolute *genius* of a designer to build a Web site for his company."

Ah. A *genius*. As opposed to Cassie's *interesting* incompetence. Becky hadn't changed a bit. But Cassie's smile didn't waver. "Well, he did the right thing, then. I'm glad it's working out for him."

Becky tossed fashionably straightened hair and gave them a blinding white smile. "Great! Oh, and *Robyn!* How *are* you? Come in, come in. *Please*. Help yourself to a drink."

Fighting regrets already, Cassie stepped inside. She surveyed the expensively appointed living room and glanced at Robyn. Robyn had her chin up. That was good. Determination was good. And she was, after all, doing this for Robyn.

Goal firmly in mind, Cassie followed Robyn to the makeshift bar for a glass of wine. Once they'd staked out a spot by the wall, Cassie turned to evaluate their prospects.

She saw a sexy, muscular-looking blonde in the corner...but tagged by a possessive red-haired female. Right. She remembered now. The girl genius from economics class, sophomore year. Which made the blonde very taken, if not married. *Such* a shame. Who else...? Three other guys, talking and laughing by the makeshift bar. Very cute. She raised an eyebrow. Definite possibilities there. She scanned over, saw a mixed group—more guys than girls—talking over Becky's CD collection. Nice. She continued surveying the rest of the room, more than pleased with the male-to-female ratio. Looked like Robyn would—

*No way.* Halting in midscan, Cassie stared at a familiar figure near the couch. Nick. Could it be? No. Well, sure, it *could* be him in the technical sense, but...*Nick? Ranger?* Cassie blinked in a futile attempt to clear her vision of what she shouldn't be seeing. And still the image remained. It really was him.

Good grief, it was almost as though she'd conjured him up herself, just by thinking about him and letting those thoughts, ever so briefly, work her hormones into a lather. Damn, if that wasn't some kind of sign, she didn't know what was. Nick, right here, right now, just out of the blue like that—

Oh, but *wow*, was that man hot. A man more tempting than sin and seven years ago, shortsighted and fuzz-brained Cassie had come *this* close to, ho, boy, embracing the bad life completely. And now, here he was, in the flesh.... What if...?

She ran a hungry gaze over his solid shoulders, powerful back, tight, tight butt. He turned slightly, glancing over his shoulder, and her gaze locked with his. Damn. The eyes. Everything else was delicious as hell...but those heavy-lidded brown eyes, with that sexy, sleepy quality to them...like dark creamy chocolate, softly melting and knowledgeable and *so* evil in such a good-bad way. A woman would want to come back for more and more.

*Breathe, Cassie. Breathe.*

Fainting would be bad. But imagine fainting at Nick Ranger's feet, in the hopes that he'd take advantage of her while she faked unconsciousness. Guilt-free, repercussion-free thrills. Wow. Kinky, no doubt, but *wow*. A girl could spin that fantasy for hours. Although, if the fantasy went as well as hoped, she probably couldn't help but "wake up" eventually....

When his lips quirked slightly, Cassie realized her quick glance had lengthened into a stare. Even worse, she watched as Nick, whose gaze never veered from hers, spoke briefly to three women who seemed to be vying for his attention. Then he turned and started walking her way, his strides long and sure. The closer he came, the more Cassie had to tilt her head back to meet his eyes. Tall. Very tall. She really liked tall.

"Oh." Becky bubbled from behind. "It's *Nick!*" She

beamed at Nick, who responded casually, his gaze only briefly leaving Cassie's.

Oh, *shit*.

"Hey, I'll bet you remember *this* guy!" Becky smiled coyly at Cassie as Nick joined them.

"Um. Sure." Cassie heard the words and could only assume they'd come from her own mouth, since no one else's was moving at the time.

"I thought so." Becky sounded smug. "Wasn't there some talk about you two—"

"Just rumor and innuendo." Nick gave a generalized grin, but his gaze still hadn't released Cassie's. "How's it going, Cassie? I haven't seen you in...seven years, maybe? A fraternity party or something."

*Or something* was right. Cassie felt her lips tremble and raised her chin slightly. "Sounds about right. How have you been, Nick?"

"Good." Thick lashes just a shade darker than his brown, almost-black hair swept lower. His expression grew even more speculative. "Better now."

Before Cassie could lose herself in dazed mumblings, Becky, of all people, rescued her. No doubt it was unintentional. "Oh, better is right! Nick here owns a *flying* school. He flies planes! He's a *pilot!* Isn't that exciting?"

Nick laughed—a little uncomfortably, or so it sounded to Cassie. "Actually, my buddies and I own it. We're partners. And it's not as exciting as it sounds. I give a lot of flying lessons, mostly to teenagers and the occasional retiree. Take on odd jobs here and there."

Becky giggled. "I heard."

"Right." Nick's grin faded. "So what have you been

up to, Cassie? Did I hear something about Web design?"

Cassie mentally shook herself. "Right. Web design. That's what I do." *Wow, such wit, Cass.*

Becky blinked with near innocence. "And I hear she makes just *oodles* of money at it, too."

*Oh, good Lord.* Cassie cringed inwardly, but was somewhat relieved by the light of hilarity in Nick's eyes. He seemed to know Becky well enough to read the story behind the words.

Well, of course he knew Becky. Given his reputation and Becky's, she'd guess he'd *known* her well and often, at least before the so-wonderful Husband stepped into the picture.

"Oodles, huh?" Nick's eyes twinkled wickedly.

"Well, I don't know about oodles, exactly..."

Dismissing Cassie's mumblings, Becky bubbled over again. "Yes, and this is Robyn Wesley."

"Hi, Robyn." Nick nodded and smiled. She smiled back.

"Robyn and Cassie work together," Becky piped up helpfully. "Robyn makes pictures and Cassie pastes them on her Web sites."

*Yes, Robyn with her crayons and I with my glue...* Sometimes Becky took the ingénue act to painful extremes.

Nick shook his head, obviously impressed despite the simplicity of Becky's description. "Sounds complicated to me. I've been thinking that I need to set up a Web site for the flight school—"

"Nick!" A clap on the shoulder halted Nick's words.

He gave the women an apologetic wave before letting the guy spin him around and redirect his attention.

After Nick moved a few reluctant steps away, Becky gave them both a cheerful smile and salute. "Must go play hostie. You girls enjoy yourselves now and don't be strangers in the future. We *love* to see old faces at these dos. The older the better."

As Becky left, Cassie and Robyn exchanged eye rolls. Apparently, two years in age was all it took to separate the cheerleaders from the senior citizens. "Do you suppose she plants those little digs on purpose or do they just slip out when she's not looking…which is *always?*"

Robyn groaned. "I honestly couldn't tell you. She must be slurping Prozac cocktails for breakfast, though. Anything that perky can't be natural."

Cassie chuckled. "You've got that right."

"So what's this about gossip and innuendo and Nick seven years ago? And how did Becky hear about it when I didn't?"

"Oh, it was nothing." Cassie waved negligently, reining her gaze away from Nick. "Just silly college stuff. Things occasionally got out of hand. You know what I mean."

"I know exactly what you mean. And that's why I'm asking."

"No big deal. Just an encounter at an off-campus fraternity party. Nick roomed with Chad Wright and Jerry…whatsisface?… Computer hacker, little guy, funny. You remember them? The party was at their place."

"Sure, I remember Jerry and Chad." Robyn waved

aside the details. "But back to Nick? Who I *didn't* know. And the encounter?"

"Was honestly no big deal."

"Which happened exactly when?" Robyn was relentless.

Cassie gave her a look but grudgingly answered. "Beginning of junior year."

Robyn tapped a finger to her chin. "Junior year...that's when you met the ex-fiancé, right? Brad, the accounting major?"

Cassie grimaced. "Well, yes. But that happened toward the end of the year. Or close to it. The frat party was way before then." She frowned, pondering chronology. "In fact, the party was right after first semester started. You transferred to Saint Louis University for the second semester, so I hadn't even met you yet. Frat party at the beginning of the year...then second semester and the design class where I met you...then Brad, also second semester. And Nick dropped out at the end of the year."

"He dropped out?"

Cassie nodded thoughtfully. "I'm not sure why. Maybe he partied himself out, but I don't know for sure. He always struck me as too smart to do something that stupid. But he left at the end of our junior year. That's all I know."

Robyn frowned. "Well, if he dropped out a semester after I transferred in, I guess it's no wonder we never met up."

"Mmm." Cassie raised her eyebrows to emphasize. "And to think, in the seven years that I've known you, I never once even mentioned Nick. See how unimportant that incident was? Absolutely the briefest of encounters."

*Oh, yeah. Way too brief and not nearly brief enough.* Laughter, dancing and harmless flirting had graduated to less-harmless touches and long kisses in his darkened bedroom. She'd lost more than one item of clothing before some self-preserving instinct persuaded her to call a panicked halt.

Perhaps her mother's persistent lectures about party boys and their rootless inclinations had sunk in, after all. *Cassie, learn from my experience. A man only hangs around while the party's hot. Come morning, he's gone with the moon and you're left with more than you can handle.* Whatever. Something had clicked, and she'd found the sense and strength to pull back before things had gone too far.

Too bad Cassie's flustered exit from the party had been public and obvious enough to incite the curiosity of twits like Becky. Apparently, Cassie disappearing with Nick into his bedroom hadn't been as sly a move as they'd hoped. Because when Cassie had made a break for it, opening the door in a flustered rush, there they'd stood, the twit and her twit following, smiling and twittering and feverishly speculating.

Faced with their knowing grins, Cassie had surrendered what remained of her dignity. She'd rushed off in social panic. Naturally her reaction had only made matters look worse. So, humiliated and quite sure her youthful resolve wouldn't stand a second testing of

Nick's charm, Cassie had avoided Nick forever after that night.

Robyn shook her head. "But why? I mean, the guy's absolutely mouthwatering. And he obviously remembers *you*."

"He is hot, isn't he?" *There* was an understatement. Cassie's insides felt all floaty and that was just from looking at the man and talking to him.

But she was over that. Perhaps not the attraction, but damn sure the near-obsession. Cassie was her own woman now, not to be ruled by wayward hormones and Nick was as wayward as a woman's hormones could get. Steadier now, Cassie spoke in a confident, almost casual tone. "Hot or not, Nick Ranger has the maturity and attention span of an eight-year-old boy."

"Not like any eight-year-old I've ever seen," Robyn countered dryly. "He looks all man to me."

"Depends on your perspective. Last I saw of him, he was just another frat boy majoring in keg parties and sorority girls. Not exactly my type of guy." Cassie silently assured herself that she wasn't lying. Not telling the whole truth, perhaps, but not lying. History was history. Nick might have inspired her fantasy life a few weak moments ago, when she let her hormones have their stubborn way with her, but she was okay now. Normal. Totally unaffected. Well, *mostly* unaffected.

"So you're saying he used women?"

Surprised, Cassie paused to refocus. "No, not really. I mean, it's true he didn't seem to stick to one girl for very long, but he *was* a lot of fun. Popular, even sweet." She shrugged. "I honestly never heard any of the girls complaining about him. They all pretty much just adored him. Even his exes. It was kind of weird." She smiled, a little wistfully. "I just thought he was like the stray cocker spaniel everyone had adopted and occasionally showered with benevolence."

"Oh, come on. You can't expect me to believe that. That man's *nobody's* object of pity. Envy maybe. Lust, definitely. Pity...oh, no. No way."

"So maybe I overstated the case a little. It was just weird that, as many women as he went through, he didn't have a sleazier reputation than he did. He got around, but nobody seemed to resent it."

Robyn cocked her head. "Okay, that is different."

"Yeah. Different." Cassie thought a moment, glanced at Nick, then back to Robyn. A sexy man who loved to play and didn't get serious. Multiple ex-girlfriends who didn't hate him after the breakup. Bingo. She hardened her resolve and rallied to the cause. "I have an idea. You and Nick."

"*Me* and Nick? Are you blind?"

"Not in the least." Cassie spoke brusquely. "Pay attention. First, we have you. A woman in need of a man who can play with her, distract her and make her feel good about herself. All without saddling her with baggage at the end of a...whatever."

Robyn snorted at the "whatever."

"I'm not finished yet." Cassie gave her a mock frown. "And then we have Nick. A man who, according to widely believed gossip, knows his way around a woman both in and out of bed, likes to have a good time and manages breakups so that no one gets hurt in the end." Cassie raised an eyebrow. "Sounds like a fling made in heaven to me. I think he's your temporary man."

Robyn gave her a doubtful look, then turned back to study Nick. She stared for a few moments, gaze ranging the hard length of his T-shirt-and-jeans-clad body. As the moment grew longer, Cassie forced her mind to go blank and concentrated on just breathing. She would not, could not—

"Well...only if you're sure you really don't want him or anything... Are you? Sure, I mean?"

Cassie spread her arms. "Positive. What do you think?"

"Uh—okay. Sure. I guess he'd be fun." Eyes overbright with nerves, Robyn turned back to Cassie. "What do I do first?"

Cassie took a deep breath and let it out slowly. "First, we keep him talking to you. I have an idea."

NICK'S PATIENCE was wearing thin. The blowhard who'd hijacked him away from Cassie—damn, but she was looking hot tonight—was still holding him hostage and mostly just to spew airplane talk and beer breath all over him.

Now, Nick had a healthy affection for beer, but this guy smelled and acted as though he'd been pickling in the stuff for several hours already. And the airplane talk was starting to wear thin. Not that Nick disliked talking about planes, either. They were his business and his passion, but this guy was obviously showing off for a girl and really just needed Nick to verify the accuracy of his every word.

"...isn' 'at right, there, Nick?"

"Hmm? Oh, sure." Appropriate answer. It had worked every time so far. Although the guy's prowess didn't seemed to impress the girl much. In fact, if she managed to brush up against *Nick's* ass just one more time, he was out of here. He had absolutely no interest in someone else's wife hitting on *him* while a third guy—still not her husband—was hitting on *her*. Nasty stuff.

"Look, I left my friends a little rudely back there, so how about if I stop monopolizing the two of you and go offer my apologies." Nick smiled at them, dodged another furtive caress and moved to rejoin Cassie and her friend.

Ignoring the slurred protests behind him, Nick waved as though not understanding then turned back to the ladies. "Sorry about that. The guy wasn't waiting or taking no for an answer."

"We sort of gathered as much." Tucking honey-colored hair behind her ear, Cassie smiled. The curve of her pretty lips kicked up a dimple in her right cheek and he stared at it. Remembering. Then she...elbowed her friend?

"Right," Robyn chimed in, a forced smile on her own face. "So. Um. Nick. You're a pilot, Becky said?"

"That's right." He smiled, nodded, his gaze passing speculatively between the two women. Something was up. Matchmaking, maybe? Hell, that would be cool. Maybe he and Cassie, finally...

Robyn's smile looked a little strained. "Uh...commercially? For an airline?"

"No, not anymore." He cheerfully played along. "Some buddies and I opened up a flight school and charter service. We rent a hangar at a small airport outside the city where we teach people to fly and take on odd jobs for private clients. We own two planes, one we bought only recently. My partners are looking into a third plane now. It'll make things tight for a while, but I think we can bring in enough business to make the investment pay off." He shifted his attention to Cassie. "Remember Chad and Jerry? From school?"

Cassie gave a crooked grin. "Sure. That's them, huh? Your partners?"

"You got it." He smiled. "Surprised?"

Cassie cocked her head. "Yes and no. I mean, I know you three hung out a lot in college. That's what I heard, I mean. Not like I actually *knew* you three or..."

She seemed to trail off, to Nick's supreme gratification. How about that? She might have blown him off after that party, but not for lack of interest. He'd wondered. She'd seemed as interested as he was at the party. Things had started to get wild between them, in fact, but then she'd gotten cold feet and seemed to dodge him at every opportunity afterward.

If all else had remained equal, he might have pressed the issue to find out what was going on with her, but then his dad's health had worsened and Nick had discovered problems bigger than his social life. Lucky for him, those problems had resolved themselves.

So now he was free to concentrate on a woman who

interested him. A woman who might even feel free to return his interest if he played his cards right. And he smelled hints of matchmaking in the air? Damn, but he was feeling lucky tonight.

Cassie cleared her throat, then continued in a stronger, more impersonal tone. "I suppose I just never considered that you three might go into business together. Especially after you left school and all...."

"Yeah. Kind of surprised us, too." Still staring at her and helpless to do otherwise, he knew he sounded distracted. He was and he didn't care. Because so was she, though she tried to hide it. Her gaze seemed to light on him and then bounce right off, as though she were afraid to let those glowing hazel eyes linger. His hopes lifted further.

Cassie looked good. Really good. She'd been pretty back in college, in a golden, all-American girl kind of way. But now all those soft lines and rounded curves had defined themselves and angled out into a Cassie that was even more intriguing.

She looked sleek and confident and sexy as hell in a purple halter dress. Like one of those gold-colored cats that might just as easily wind herself contentedly around a guy's legs as scratch him bloody. All depending on his behavior and her mood. Now, generally, he considered himself a dog kind of guy, but for Cassie, he'd be more than happy to make an exception.

"So...it's a new business, then?" She seemed to be forcing a focus.

"The flight school? Relatively. We started up about a year ago, but we're still getting our feet under us."

She nodded.

"Yeah, now that you mention it, we really do need to get a Web site up and running. So far, word of mouth has worked for us, but a Web site's almost a necessity these days." Suddenly inspired, he tried for a casual tone. He was a little rusty at this stuff. "So, would you, by any chance, have time to take on a new client?" He grinned, projecting every ounce of boyish charm he could manage. "Like, for example, a new flying school and chartering company?"

She blinked, wide-eyed, as though he'd done his level best to yank the rug out from under her. Robyn snorted and broke off a chuckle, which distracted him only briefly. Cassie cleared her throat. "Um, sure. I mean, I'm always looking for new clients. I thought you'd be building your own site, though. Isn't Jerry a whiz with computers?" She glanced at Robyn before returning her attention to Nick. "I was actually going to suggest that Robyn help you...if you haven't come up with a logo yet, that is. She's great with that stuff."

"I'm sure she is. So, if I hire you as my, um, *Web* mistress, don't I get her, too?" He gave her a teasing grin to bypass her unexpected skittishness. Perhaps he'd been off base with the matchmaking theory? Still, he was sure he'd seen interest in Cassie's eyes.

Robyn laughed and answered for Cassie. "Oh, sure. Cass usually offers a two-fer deal. But not to just *anyone.*"

Nick laughed outright. "Excellent."

"But—" Cassie was looking a little wide-eyed now.

"Don't you want to see some of my work before you hire me?"

He shrugged. "I'm assuming you have a portfolio?"

"Of course."

"So I'll check it out."

"Oh. Well, here, then." Cassie fished out her card and handed it to him. "My Web site address is on here. You can access my portfolio from there, if you want to take a peek."

Nick studied it with interest. "Nice card. No physical address?"

"Not necessary. I have a phone number and e-mail. That's how I do business."

He nodded. "You work out of your apartment, then?"

"Sure."

"All of your work? You're not affiliated with another company or organization?"

"Just me. And Robyn, of course. You won't regret a thing once you see her work, by the way. She's an awesome artist. Really. In fact—" she cast an encouraging smile between Robyn and Nick "—you two should really get together and work out some sort of theme or image you're trying to promote so she can get a general idea for appropriate graphics and illustrations."

Glancing between Cassie and Robyn, he arrived at unexpected conclusion number two. Not about to be sidetracked, he smiled and moved in closer to Cassie. "But I'd probably need to discuss that with you, too, though, right?"

Spilling her drink slightly and only on her hand, Cassie stepped aside to set her wineglass down on a table, then turned back. The whole maneuver managed to insert a little distance between them. Smooth, but transparent. She picked up a napkin and wiped off her hand. Maintaining the distance.

"Sure." Her gaze flickered to and away from his. "But you and Robyn could discuss it first, get a feel for the artistic vision, and then we could all sit down and work out the details."

"Do you always have your digital artist conduct business for you?" He worded it as a question, even forced a mild expression on his face, but he could tell that Cassie recognized a challenge when she heard it. He wasn't about to let her pawn him off on Robyn.

"No, and that's not what we're doing. It's just a matter of practicality. You want to see what kind of site we could build for you, right? Well, she's the artist and I'm the techie. I have an eye for organization and design, and I'm the one you'd ordinarily deal with for business matters and site maintenance, but my designs have to flow with her artistry." She shrugged. "I thought you might like a more visual idea of your site before we settle down to business."

"Right." He flashed his most effective smile. "But I'm a techie myself, in many ways. I guess I'd prefer it if the technical side was primary and the art sort of worked into the site after the fact." He nodded an apology at Robyn. "Not to discount the quality of your work. I have faith that you could create something snazzy to go with whatever design Cassie and I decide is most appropriate for my business." He turned up the wattage, but considered it basically unnecessary at this point.

Robyn was already glancing between him and Cassie with a knowing expression on her face. Cassie might have some misguided notions of pairing, but Robyn knew which way the wind blew. Toward Cassie. "No offense taken. I think you and Cassie ought to meet up as soon as possible."

When Cassie started to interrupt, Nick just smiled wider. "Great idea. I was thinking the same thing myself. How's Tuesday, Cassie? Care to meet me for lunch?"

"Lunch?"

"Or coffee? If that's more convenient."

"But—"

"She's free." Robyn spoke with quiet efficiency. "There's a coffee shop near her apartment, in fact, if that's convenient for you. I can give you the address."

"Robyn!" Cassie spoke in a furious whisper that Robyn cordially ignored.

"Great. So...just so I know, is there anyone I should watch out for? A man who might get jealous if I'm seen having coffee with you?" Fighting laughter now—the byplay between the two women was highly entertaining—Nick gave Cassie an innocent look. She was so cute and provokable; a guy couldn't resist provoking. So he was fishing. Obviously. And, even more obviously, he expected his new ally to jump in wherever necessary.

She did. "Nope," Robyn piped up sweetly. "She's not seeing anyone seriously—unless you count the computer monitor that's been attached to her nose. She's free as a bird.''

Cassie groaned, her face burning.

Two minutes later, the details settled mostly to Nick's and Robyn's satisfaction, Nick excused himself with a grin.

And Cassie was left to wonder just when and how she'd managed to lose control of this situation. She now had a cozy business date with Robyn's temporary man? Her own hormonal nemesis? Not good. Really not good.

# _____Step 3_____

### *The Setup*
*We commit ourselves to the mad ingenuity*
*of said savvy girlfriend.*

HALF PANICKED, Cassie dragged a grinning Robyn through Becky's living room and out the front door.

Robyn inhaled deeply of the night air. "Mmm. Much better. Becky's house is nice, but it wouldn't have hurt her to open a window and let some air in."

"*Air?* What are you talking about?" Cassie, flustered and frustrated, almost screeched the last.

Robyn chuckled. "Remember Becky's allergies? She never opens windows. That's why it was so stifling in there."

"Hello? Robyn? Forget Becky and her allergies and her stuffy house. What's gotten into *you?*" Cassie gave Robyn an exasperated look. "Nick's supposed to be *your* temporary man, remember?" Widening her eyes, she leaned confidingly closer, seeking comprehension somewhere, anywhere. She continued in a sarcastic singsong. "But Nick's not going to realize his good fortune if you and he are never alone together. Sheer logistics, Robyn. You gotta get to know the guy, without me hanging around."

Breezily ignoring exasperation, sarcasm and mockery, Robyn just wrinkled her nose. "Frankly, Cassie, I think Nick preferred having *you* all to himself, although I noticed you did manage to include me as a fifth wheel in your little meeting. Over my objections. And his, too, I'm sure."

"He's just acting on what's familiar right now." Cassie waved a dismissive hand. "Once he gets to know *you* better—"

"Give it up, Cassie. Nick's after *your* bones, not mine."

Cassie rolled her eyes. "Nick's after the easiest bones he can find. At the moment, yours are supposed to be *easier* than mine. Remember?"

"Cassie!" Still, Robyn dissolved into outraged laughter.

Cassie grinned a little herself. "You know what I mean. You have to make yourself available. You didn't. You put me between you two and that's not going to accomplish anything."

Robyn raised an eyebrow. "If Nick has his way it will."

"Well, he won't, at least not with me, so it's a moot point. Let me repeat myself. You have to make yourself available. Otherwise, no dice."

Robyn glanced at her and then away. "I'm not sure I can do that."

"Because of Alex."

Robyn shrugged. "I'm just not *emotionally* available yet. It's as simple as that."

Cassie closed her eyes on an instinctive wince. Appropriate or not, the term "emotionally available" was just too much talk-show psychobabble to stomach.

And completely unlike Robyn. Cassie opened her eyes. Which meant Robyn was panicking and wielding catch phrases for excuses. Busted.

"Come off it, Robyn. This is as simple as mind over matter." Cassie raised her brows and leveled Robyn with her best cut-the-crap stare. "And you are so available. At least, available enough for someone like Nick. I'm serious, Robyn. He won't tie your heart up in knots or expect huge emotional leaps from you. In fact, I think he'd help you get over Alex better than any other guy I can name right now."

"And why is that?" Robyn gave her a curious though doubting glance.

Cassie smiled just a little. "Because he's one of that awesome breed of guy. The kind who just adores women, gets a kick out of all our habits and goofy quirks, loves to flirt for the sake of flirting. You know what I mean? Sure, there are guys who date a lot, go through a lot of women, but when it comes down to it, they don't really respect them or even like just hanging around them."

Robyn nodded, listening intently now.

"But Nick's not like that. He really just appreciates women. And you can tell that by being around him and seeing how he operates. I think he'd do lovely things for your ego and your sex life. He'd also be a good person to compare to Alex. What's the last nice thing Alex ever said to you? To make you feel good about yourself."

Robyn scowled. "You only think the worst of Alex."

"You bet I do," Cassie shot back. "I hate the way he treats you."

"Alex says nice things to me. He just gets absorbed in his work sometimes."

"You're in denial again—and that's exactly my point." Cassie lowered her brows. "You need perspective. And I think you can get that by spending time with a guy like Nick."

"If Nick is so wonderful, why aren't you jumping him yourself?"

"You're the one who needs a temporary man, not me." Cassie glanced away.

"And you're so sure that's all Nick could be for you. A temporary man. A brief fling."

"As I understand it, that's all Nick could be for *any* woman. But it would be a *fun* fling. Good memories, just short ones. You need that." Cassie gently bumped Robyn's arm, gave her an encouraging smile.

Robyn looked wary still. "Maybe."

"Think about it, Robyn. I mean, when's the last time you had fun, uncomplicated sex?"

"Cassie!"

Cassie gave Robyn a no-nonsense look. "Answer the question."

Robyn huffed, fidgeted a little, then tossed up a hand. "I don't know." She folded her arms across her chest, eyes blinking rapidly, and continued in a low, emotion-thickened voice. "Alex gets...*absorbed*. In his work. He says I distract him. Sex with me distracts him from his art. So it's been a while since we actually..."

Cassie stared. "Is this guy for real?" When Robyn

turned with the obvious intent of stalking off, Cassie gently grabbed her arm. "Sorry. I'm *sorry*. I just can't believe he'd do that to you. It's so selfish. And hurtful."

Robyn stared at the ground for a moment and then shrugged. "Okay, you're right. It did hurt. I admit it. I felt like he didn't really want me sometimes, though he swore that it was just the opposite. That he wanted me *too* much."

Cassie studied her. "That's something, I guess. But still. It's not healthy. You couldn't have been happy with the way things were."

"No, it's not. And I wasn't." Robyn's voice was small. She took a deep breath and spoke a little louder. "I think it's just that, with Alex, everything has to be so *intense*. Everything. Every time, always."

Cassie barely held back a retort. Intense was putting it mildly. Alex's mood swung regularly between depression and euphoria. Cassie couldn't imagine dealing with that on a daily basis, but Robyn seemed utterly enthralled by it. Addicted to it, even. Cassie thought both of them needed to learn to *chill*, for heaven's sake. Living on the edge of a nervous breakdown must be so exhausting. Intense.

*Intense? Everything?* Cassie blinked in lurid curiosity. "Even the sex was intense?"

"Oh, wow, yeah. Not often enough, but when it was..." Robyn shook her head. "It was exciting. Thrilling." She sounded breathless.

*Addicting.* "But not really...fun?"

Robyn paused, her throat working a little before she responded. "He always expects everything to be a *meaningful* experience. That's hard to sustain in a relationship, you know? Sometimes I just wanted to play and laugh with him. To relax and have fun. We used to do that. Early on." She paused, then continued in a low tone, as though uttering something she shouldn't. "If you want to know the ugly truth...I think fun, uncomplicated, laid-back...*sex*...sounds wonderful right now. It's been so long. I just wish I could have had that with Alex."

"I know, honey." She squeezed Robyn's arm. "Don't you worry, though. Dr. Cassie to the rescue. We'll get you a fun guy with laughs and good times to spare. You need to get laid before something withers and falls off."

Robyn choked. "Withers? What *withers?*"

"Let's not find out." Turning, Cassie slung an arm over Robyn's shoulder and began walking toward her car. "I've heard that Nick once made a woman yodel under the stadium bleachers. Imagine something good enough to make you yodel. Horizontally." She shook her head in wonder, trying not to imagine it herself.

She could believe it, though. That was the hell of it. Nick was probably phenomenal in bed. Just fantasizing about the possibilities was enough to reduce her to cold sweats and mental stutterings. Sometimes she really regretted foregoing the real-life experience after that fraternity party seven years ago.

But sex at a frat party had seemed as low as she could go. Especially with the king of the frat boys. And Nick had been that. He'd partied harder than all of them put together, until he'd left college after his junior year.

She'd lost track of him at that point and refused to admit aloud how much she'd wondered about him since then. Too humiliating.

"WEB SITE? WHAT THE HELL do we need with a Web site?" Chad grumbled over his coffee.

"Join the twenty-first century, why don't you?" Jerry murmured with benign contempt.

Chad snorted.

"Jerry's right, Chad. Anyone who's anyone or hopes to *be* anyone in business, has a presence on the Internet. That's where busy people go to find what they want— and what they're willing to pay for." Nick gave him a meaningful look. "We want to be there when someone comes looking for services like ours."

"Well, that makes sense, I guess. But how the hell are we going to do that? I guess Jerry—"

"No, we need Jerry doing his job, not working on a Web site." Jerry nodded in agreement and Nick continued. "I already have a Web designer in mind. Cassandra Smythe. Ring a bell?"

"Cassandra Smythe?" Chad's focus narrowed. "That wouldn't be the same Cassie Smythe you drooled over back in college, would it?"

"Same one. I can't believe you remembered. Guess the beer didn't kill all those brain cells of yours."

"Hey, you kegged with the best of us, buddy." He glanced at Nick. "So what's up with Cassie? I seem to recall you wanting her pretty bad."

Nick shrugged. "I had it bad for a lot of girls in school. You know that."

"Do we ever," Chad chortled, and elbowed Jerry.

"Yeah, man. Do you remember the one about Diane? Yodeling under the bleachers? *Damn.*" Jerry whooped and Chad laughed even louder.

"Nick Ranger's my heeee-ro." Jerry mocked him in a nasally falsetto, then shook his head. "You and the women, Nick. That was somethin' else."

"Knock it off, guys." Damn, not that one again. Old and too often told story—and it all grew more outrageous every time they told it. Given all the tales they spun about his partying college days, you'd have thought he'd spent eight years there instead of three short ones. Until his dad got sick and Nick had left SLU to get a job to ease the financial burden on his family. He'd had fun in college, but he didn't regret any of the decisions he'd made since then, either.

In fact, he was proud of his accomplishments, though a lot of his old college friends didn't acknowledge anything beyond his failure to get his degree. Or else they downplayed what he'd accomplished in favor of the legend he'd been or the one that he'd become. From college party boy to cowboy in the sky, with nothing substantial in between.

Considering a lot of college grads never figured out what they really wanted out of life, Nick didn't consider his lack of a degree to be meaningful at all. Instead of the bachelor's in engineering he'd originally sought—with some ambivalence—he'd attained his pilot's license and certification. He'd logged enough flight time to be rated for commercial flying and more, attended some business classes to aid his current venture, before teaming up with Chad and Jerry to start a business. A business that he loved and took very seriously.

Still absently skimming the logs, Nick frowned at a sudden thought. "Hey, who has the Drummond job this morning?"

Chad groaned. "Tell me it's someone else's turn."

"Quit whining. Nick and I both have new students scheduled for today. Besides, I had the Drummonds last time. And Nick here had to take 'em up twice before that. Your turn to step up."

"I swear to God it's the last time."

Juggling logs and schedules, Nick ran a finger down a column of numbers and shook his head. "Maybe, maybe not. It's good money. And you know we need all the business we can get. Drummonds want us, Drummonds get us."

Jerry laughed. "That's not the tune you were singing when it was *your* turn to take 'em up."

Nick grinned crookedly. "So it's not my turn." He clapped Chad on the shoulder. "Let my good buddy Chad do all the bitching this time."

Chad scowled. "While you get to go talk Cassie out of her pants."

Nick shoved him. "Don't be an ass. Cassie's not the type."

"Then she sure as hell isn't *your* type, is she?" On that parting shot, Chad got to his feet and stalked off to ready the plane for the Drummonds.

Still laughing at his friend's disgruntled wit, Jerry propped his boots on Nick's desk. "So, what's the call, Nick? Is she your type or not?"

Nick shoved the feet off, more annoyed than he wanted to admit. "Maybe so. Maybe not. I'm not a kid anymore. Think it's possible that I might want to date a woman for real this time?"

He'd swear the guys had aged seven years right along with him, but apparently not. They still acted like horn-dog college kids. He used to be there. Back then, he'd been every bit as single-minded as his friends. A different woman every month, sometimes every week. There were so many and he'd had so damn much fun with every one of them.

But now, he couldn't remember the last time—okay, about two months ago—he'd been on a date. Minor. Very minor. Before that...Shannon, he guessed. They'd dated for several months, but it had been really casual, exactly what he'd needed at the time. They hadn't broken up so much as just drifted in different directions, no hard feelings and, he'd swear, well-wishing on both sides.

Yep. Chad and Jerry would laugh themselves sick if they knew how lame his love life really was these days. Until lately, he'd had to be married to his planes to keep the business afloat and his bills paid.

Sure, his buddies had contributed a stake and a considerable number of hours to the business, but most of the worrying and dreaming and hoping had been his. Chad and Jerry were happy enough to be here now, but all three of them knew this wasn't a forever deal. Eventually, as each guy figured out what he wanted in life, Nick would end up buying him out. It was understood.

Nick's goal now was to be able to offer them a hefty

profit and good memories for their time, cash and trouble. He owed them that and more.

"So you're serious about Cassie?"

"Huh?" Nick looked up in mild alarm.

Jerry smirked. "I mean, about her building us a Web site."

"Oh. Yeah, I think she'd do a great job. I have a meeting with her today—" he checked his watch "—a few hours from now. So I spent some time last night checking out other sites she's built, and they looked great. I'd like to see what she could do for us."

Jerry shrugged a shoulder. "Go for it, then."

Nick grinned. "That's the plan."

"NICK." CASSIE STEPPED back in surprise. Sure, it was Tuesday. And despite her personal misgivings, she'd planned on meeting him and Robyn at the coffeehouse as scheduled, but here he was half an hour early...and at her apartment. She frowned. "How'd you get my address?"

"I called Becky this morning. She gave it to me." He gave her an innocent look. "Is that a problem? I thought you'd be able to show me stuff better on your computer here than at the coffeehouse."

"Oh. Sure. But we're meeting Robyn...."

He smiled. "How about we call her and have her meet us here? Or we could always walk over for coffee after we finish on the computer."

"Um. I guess. Sure." Taking a deep breath, she tried for professional composure—a near impossibility. Forcing her attention to stay trained on a deadline project yesterday and its follow-up today had taken every ounce of focus she'd possessed. She hadn't had time to prepare and bolster her position. "I know Robyn's finishing up a lunch appointment right now, so it's probably best just to meet her at the coffeehouse in half an hour."

"Great." He gave her an easy smile. Then gestured. "May I...?"

"Oh, sure. Come in." She stepped back, glancing around, and kicked an empty pizza box under the couch, then discreetly snatched up a bra and stuffed it under a cushion. "It's kind of a mess. I've been working under deadline...."

He seemed to be fighting a grin. "No problem."

Nope, no problem at all. Half an hour. She couldn't damage much in half an hour, right? "So. Nick. What do you want your Web site to say?"

He frowned, bemused, then shook his head and laughed. "I don't know. Hire me? Use me? Pay me money?"

He looked so boyish and genuine, and just so damned cute, she couldn't help a responding chuckle. "Subtlety's a delicate art."

"My pitch needs work, huh?"

"A bit." She gave him a wry look and waved him into the tiny extra bedroom she used as an office. "Have a seat."

Unlike her living room, the office was almost painfully neat. Her equipment was state-of-the-art and she was a stickler for paperwork and order.

"Nice office."

"Thanks."

"Actually, your whole apartment building is pretty cool. The layout's different."

Cassie smiled. "Yeah, I thought so, too. It just sort of called out to me when I was house hunting last winter. Then, when I found this apartment sublet for way less than I was willing to pay—" she shrugged "—I just knew it was meant to be. And as fate would have it, the couple leasing it moved permanently just a few months later. So now it's mine. A bit pricier, but I can afford it now that I have some steady clients."

"Lucky break."

Her smile widened. "Yeah, fate can be kind occasionally."

"Fate, huh?" He gave her a curious grin.

She just shrugged. "Sure. So let's talk Web sites."

"Okay." While she turned to face the monitor, he leaned in, elbows on his knees, to peer over her shoulder.

Feeling his breath brush her shoulder and neck, raising thousands of miniscule hairs on sensitive skin, Cassie stilled. After a moment, when she was pretty sure she could manipulate the mouse without trembling or otherwise making a fool of herself, she did so. *Click.* "We have some options. I guess it all depends on your priorities."

"Like?"

She inhaled sharply. Did the man need to lean so close? Probably. She grumbled silently. Not fair. Web sites. Let's think Web sites. Preferably not of the X-rated variety that issued regular spam invitations to her electronic mailbox. *Hi. My name is Cassie. Want to join me and my Web cam for some techie sex? I do HTML...*

*Ugh. Get a grip, Cass.*

"Options. Yes." She cleared her throat. "You could..." She clicked past a page, then moved on to another. She'd built this page last year for a friend who sold homemade scents and candles on the Internet. "This one's classy yet direct. We lead right in with the sales pitch and hot deals. It's simple but effective...."

She clicked through to yet another, more recently built Web site. "Of course, there's also the surprise tactic, if that's the kind of thing you're going for. It's riskier. The idea is to catch a surfer's attention and pique his interest before leading him into the site...like this."

"Hmm." Nick's voice was a low rumble over her shoulder, but she felt it vibrate down her spine. Goose bumps rose along her arms. Damn it anyhow, his voice was giving her goose bumps. Unacceptable. She shifted in her chair, scooting it slightly to the side, a maneuver he could easily mistake for courtesy to allow him a better view of the screen.

"What do you think?" She murmured the question.

He reached past her for the mouse, raising an eyebrow for permission.

"Be my guest." So much for her distancing maneuver.

He scooted in closer, bracing his forearm on the back of her chair. If she leaned back, she'd be sliding almost right into his arms. Temptation. Resist, idiot, *resist*.

And exactly *why* did she agree to do this again? Alone in her apartment with a man like Nick? But it was just the one meeting. Surely that's all it would take to settle everything for now. A simple, half hour *pre*-meeting meeting.

Dazed and half panicked, she watched Nick click through the Web site, then pull up the next and the one following. He efficiently skimmed through each one before returning to the second site she'd discussed with him. The one that played on surprise. The riskier one.

"I like this idea."

"You're sure." She gave him a cautioning look. "I haven't tracked this particular site for very long, so I don't know how successful it's been."

"That's okay." He murmured distractedly, his attention fixed thoughtfully on the screen. "This concept works. Jives with our image. Yeah, this is it." He glanced at her, a grin tugging at his mouth. "I have sort of a cowboy-in-the-sky reputation. It's a little exaggerated, but it brings in business."

"But you didn't earn it. The cowboy image." She gave him a skeptical look.

He shrugged. "Doesn't much matter, does it?"

"I guess not." She stared thoughtfully at him. "Cowboy in the sky. How do you earn a reputation like that and still live to hear about it?" It was a rhetorical question.

He grinned and took it as such, then turned back to the monitor. "This sort of impact fits the image, though, don't you think?"

She followed his gaze. "Given the proper graphics and imagery...maybe a small, edgy-looking plane seeming to approach and fly directly at the viewer, before...yeah, I think so. Yes." She nodded decisively. "And Robyn thrives on artistic challenge. She's gonna love you for this one."

"Oh. Great." He glanced sideways at Cassie. "What about you?"

She gave him a wry grin and he laughed. "Don't say it, whatever you're thinking. It can only hurt me." He paused while she chuckled. "I was actually referring to the challenge part. What turns you on in Web design?"

It was a sincere question, she realized, so she thought for a moment. "I'm not sure. It's hard to describe." She shrugged. "I mean, I like that it's a nice blend of logical and creative thought. So I guess that means both sides of the brain get a decent workout." She smiled a little, thinking about it. "And, occasionally, an effect or graphic I've programmed turns out slightly different than I intended. Sometimes, it's even better or it gives me an idea for something even better. That's fun."

She tipped her head. "Yes, I enjoy all of it, but I'd have to say it's the occasional inspirations that really do it for me."

He nodded slowly and she studied his thoughtful expression. "How about you? Why flying? Why flight school and this odd-job stuff over commercial flying?"

He turned to stare into the screen again, his fingers absently twirling a lock of her hair that had draped itself over the back of her chair. "Flying was something I dreamed about when I was growing up." His lips quirked at the memory. "Just another kid fantasy, you know? Firefighter, superhero, pilot..."

She nodded, trying to ignore the gentle tug of his fingers in her hair. His arm was still on the back of her chair and he was just using his fingertips to caress and tug at the strands. She'd swear he wasn't even aware that he was doing it and yet she could feel each tug arrowing straight to her lower belly. It was enough to drive a woman batty with lust.

His eyes distant, Nick continued his story. "I even took flying lessons in high school and college, but I always just thought that flying could only be a hobby. That I could fly on weekends and vacations, but would have to work a regular job during the week. Then, after I left SLU, I started working this job by the airport." His fingers stilled.

"It was just a drone job, something to support myself while I got my act together. Anyway, at lunch, I'd drive to this deserted lot and park there to sit and watch the planes take off and land. And I remembered how cool it was to be the one piloting the plane. How much I'd missed it. So I went back to it. Logged hours when I could. Then one day I turned around and discovered I actually had a healthy savings account, but I still hated the drone job. So, I took a chance. Somebody had to make a living flying, so I figured what the hell? It might as well be me." He shrugged.

"What about Chad and Jerry? How did they figure in?"

He shrugged, his shoulder brushing gently against her shoulder blade. "They were kind of directionless after college. Didn't really like their majors." He chuckled. "Chad still doesn't know why he got the poli-sci degree. Works for some people, but not for him. Jerry was pretty much in the same boat. Anyway, I sort of twisted their arms into taking flying lessons with me and logging some big-time hours of their own. Turned out they liked it almost as much as I did. Lucky break, huh?"

She smiled. "Lucky breaks all around."

He tugged on her hair. "You said it."

"But couldn't you make more money flying commercially?"

"Oh, I did. I got my commercial pilot's certification." He shrugged, a puzzled smile quirking his lips. "Along with the flight lessons and all those hours logged, the three years of prep and engineering classes helped more than I thought they would. Anyway, once I was qualified, I flew smaller craft for one of the minor airlines for about six months."

He cocked his head. "And it was okay. Great, in fact. I mean, I liked the flying part, of course, and you can't beat a steady paycheck. But I really wanted to be my own boss or at least partner in a company with some guys I trust. So, Chad, Jerry and I pooled our cash and our qualifications, went into debt up to our necks..."

"And...here you are?"

"To make a long story short...yep. Here I am. Mostly poor but solvent and doing what I want to do."

"Flying your own planes." She murmured it, more impressed than she thought she'd be. Playboy or not, the man had some serious dreams and wasn't afraid of chasing after them.

"Flying my own planes." His eyes, deepening to a dark chocolate, seemed to pull her in. He was so close, that half embrace nearly surrounding her shoulders. The look he was giving her. She turned slightly, only vaguely aware that she did so, and slid a hand closer, knocking against the mouse.

*Click.* Their gazes snapped to his hand, still clutching the mouse and then to the screen. *Whirrrr...*

"Oh, damn. Did I..." Nick released the mouse and scooted aside to make room for her. Those maddening fingers finally freed her hair.

"No. It's okay." She laughed a little shakily. A close call, indeed, but not in the way he was suggesting. "Really. It just closed out the program, but I have it all saved on disk and hard drive. No big deal."

He gave her a sheepish grin. "I know Excel and some basic data and word processing, but I'm afraid I'm less than ept with the fancy design stuff."

She chuckled, as intended, then glanced discreetly at the time. "Oh, shoot. We were supposed to meet Robyn ten minutes ago and I didn't even get all my information from you. Services you offer, what you charge, all that good stuff—"

"No big deal. I have paperwork I can give you that summarizes everything." He smiled, then offered her a hand up.

Disarmed by the gesture—unexpected, even gentlemanly?—she accepted the hand then awkwardly maneuvered her way toward her bag and the door. "I hope she hasn't been waiting too long...."

Using tardiness as an excuse to rush the trip from apartment to coffee shop, she speed-walked most of the way. Nick's easy strides kept up to her pace without visible effort on his part. When he held the door open for her and allowed her to pass, she made a beeline for Robyn. Her friend was sitting at a table by herself, grinning and watching their approach.

After a brief explanation for their tardiness, Cassie lowered her brows and smiled curiously at Robyn. "Okay, what? *What?* You've obviously been giggling somewhere inside that crazy head of yours since we walked in here. What's the joke?"

Robyn snorted and chuckled outright. "Okay, okay. I wasn't sure Nick would want this discussed at our serious business meeting...."

Nick grinned. "Don't let me stop you."

"You asked for it, then. I just ran into your buddy Chad outside this little burger place near the airport. He was coming, I was going, that kind of thing. So we stopped to chat, and—" She laughed again. "Oh, God, I never thought I'd see the day when that guy blushed. He was always such a dog, you know?"

Nick just closed his eyes for a moment then gave Robyn a patient, rueful look. Robyn chortled.

Cassie glanced between them, feeling like the odd man out. It was sort of the point of this whole endeavor, but— "I don't get it. Why would a plane make Chad blush...?" Something started to click. Surely not.

Nick pinched the bridge of his nose, grimacing. "Chad knows he's not supposed to discuss clients."

Robyn waved it off. "I don't think he could help himself. The poor guy looked traumatized. The Drummonds?"

Nick gave in and nodded. "It was his first time up with them."

"And?" Cassie prodded him on with word and look.

"Well, let's just say that it's not exactly the mile-high club, but this couple gets pretty damn close."

Nick's cheeks looked just the slightest bit flushed.

"No way." Cassie started laughing. "Oh, my God. You can't mean these people actually—"

Robyn snorted with laughter. When a cell phone jingled shrilly, Robyn glanced at her purse and looked supremely torn. "Oh, damn it. I want to stay and listen, but I've been waiting for this call...." Cursing and still laughing, she retrieved her phone and slipped from her seat to go outside.

Turning her gaze back to Nick's ruddy cheeks, Cassie grinned tauntingly and motioned him onward. "Come on. You can't just leave it at that. What? I take it you guys fly some couple in your plane and they..."

Nick dropped his face into his hands, scrubbed at his cheeks for a moment, then gestured helplessly. "What can I do? My folks have been friends with the Drummonds for years. When they first asked me to fly them to an airport near this condo they own by the lake, I just thought it was a good gig. No big deal. Maybe they were even just helping me out, when they could have driven or taken a commercial jet just as easily. But...well, anyway, they sort of make a habit of commencing their vacation early."

"You mean they—"

He nodded. "Sort of. Mostly. Yeah."

"Right in front of you?"

"Well, we were in the Cessna—it's a four-seater—so mostly behind me. I'm sure chauffeurs and cabdrivers put up with it all the time, but the Drummonds were the first for me." He winced at the memory. "And I've known them since I was a kid. It's like knowing my folks or my grandparents are going at it. Just a few feet away from me."

Cassie choked. "Just...like that. Right there. Ho, boy." She slumped back in her seat, laughing.

He grimaced. "Yeah. Just the lead-up, though, not the act. Not that I've noticed anyway—and I tend to think I would. I did manage to strong-arm Chad and Jerry into taking turns so I don't have to see it all the time, though." He closed his eyes briefly. "God, I wonder if my parents have any clue..."

Cassie shook her head slowly, highly entertained. And enlightened. "So party boy cowboy in the sky blushes at the very idea."

He gave her a disgruntled look. "Hey, I like sex as much as the next guy. Doesn't mean I want it going on in the back seat of my airplane."

"You said they didn't get that far."

"And that's the *only* reason I keep taking them up."

She studied him, smiling slightly.

"What?" He shot her a suspicious look from under wrinkled brows.

"I love it." She smiled wickedly at him. "This prudish side of you. When did you grow that?"

He raised both brows for emphasis. "This is not prudishness. This is just good taste and good business sense. We're talking about my planes, here."

"Ah. They're sacred?"

"You got it. I like kink. Kink's great. Anytime you want kink, I'm your guy. But not in my plane." He grimaced. "And maybe I don't want it foisted on me by pseudo-relatives, either. There's something unnatural about that."

She cracked up again. "Come on, Nick. Don't even try to tell me some girl hasn't seduced you in that plane of yours."

"Nope. The plane is unmolested. I swear it."

"What about Chad and—"

He shook his head. "I'd nail 'em to the wall for it and they know it."

"Well." She gave him a speculative look.

"'Well' is right." He looked out of sorts for a moment, before narrowing his eyes at her. "You're enjoying this just a little too much, Miss Wholesome. So when did *you* grow a dirty mind?"

"Hey, every red-blooded woman has a dirty mind. We just don't let it out to play all the time." She raised a superior eyebrow at him.

He chuckled. "Damn. I wish I'd known that when we got together at that college party. I might've—"

Robyn slid into her seat with a whoosh. "Good. I got rid of him. So, what'd I miss?"

Oh. God. Saved at the very last second by her very best friend in the whole, wide world. Cassie barely resisted fanning herself. Good grief, to have to go from the titillating mile-high couple to dirty minds and reminiscences of near seduction. With Nick. Not just fantasy Nick, but reality Nick. Who was still looking at her with heat and possibilities in his heavy-lidded gaze.

*No.* Oh, no. She was *not* falling under his spell again. No how, no way. She was so over him. She had to be. History. The man was history. No more.

"Robyn." Cassie's voice was a little high-pitched, but not trembling, at least. "You're back. Anyone important? On the phone, I mean?"

"Another client, but—"

Cassie, desperate for innocent levity, gave Robyn a shaming look. "But I'm your only *important* client."

Robyn grinned. "Yes, you are, dear. Now, I missed—"

"—*most* of the business meeting between Nick and me." With a smile for both of them, Cassie segued less than smoothly from the mile-high club to Nick's Web site.

As expected, however, Robyn was immediately enthusiastic, and Nick, thank God, was at least partially distracted from the undercurrents still heating the air between him and Cassie. While listening to Nick and Robyn work out some of the artistic details and jumping in here and there to provide logistical input, Cassie tried desperately to erase the mental images that seemed to form and intertwine without her permission.

Still, she couldn't help but wonder what it would take to persuade Nick into an in-flight—or at least, *in-plane*—seduction. Surrendering to it would probably equate to a lifetime commitment in his eyes. No doubt those planes of his would go permanently unmolested. What a rotten shame.

# _____ Step 4 _____

_The Bar Crawl_
_We take fearless inventory of available, if sleazy options._

"OKAY. I WASN'T READY before, but I'm really, _really_ ready now."

Cassie started at the sound and tried to mentally catch up. For several minutes she'd been lost in a replay of Tuesday's business meeting, imagining where it might have led if she hadn't ended her part by pleading other commitments. But she'd left Nick with Robyn and then... "Robyn?"

Robyn, who'd just flung open the door on an outburst of speech, kicked it closed behind her and started pacing the room. "I mean it, Cassie. Let's do it. Now."

"Do what? What's going on? Did something happen?"

"You know what I mean." Robyn waved a hand with agitated impatience. "The...the _dating_ thing. I want a temporary guy and I want him now."

"O-kaay?" Cassie rose from the kitchen chair and studied her friend more closely. Robyn had tears shining in her eyes, only this time they looked like angry tears. "You're upset. What's wrong?"

"Nothing." Robyn averted her eyes and continued

pacing. "You just talked me into this temporary-man thing. That's all."

"Bull. Talk to me. Something happened." Robyn looked up again, and Cassie caught her breath. "*Alex.* You ran into him, didn't you."

"More like he ran into me." Robyn was hissing and ready to spit now. "Or right *over* me."

"Not a pleasant encounter, I take it."

"You could say that. He wanted me to know that he'd take me back whenever I was through pouting. Just that I should take care to schedule any future dramas around the upcoming week. He says he's preparing for a show and doesn't need my *small-minded histrionics* to distract him from his work."

"What an ass."

"That's what *I* called him. With the addition of a few adjectives."

*Yes!* Cassie mentally pumped an arm straight into the air. "Good for you, Robyn. Boy, did he have that coming."

"Yes, he did." Robyn was looking even more pumped than Cassie—but not with jubilation. The woman looked truly vengeful. Her eyes glittered with it. "And now I'm ready to take my...my *small-minded histrionics* on the town. And get them well and truly *laid*."

"Oh. Kay." So maybe she'd pumped Robyn just a little too much? No, Alex had done that with the histrionics crack. And everything preceding it. So what now? Stall until Robyn rediscovered sanity? Possibly. "I guess that could be a plan."

"You bet it's a plan. I think you've had the right idea all along, Cass. I should have listened."

Cassie flinched. "Um, about that idea..."

Robyn halted, arms akimbo, brow raised and her impatience palpable.

Cassie backpedaled. "Look, even if we went out...I couldn't promise that we'd actually run into Nick. But if you waited a few days, maybe a week even, I could set something up. Something comfortable and casual so you could ease into—"

"No."

Given Robyn's present state of mind, Cassie had already figured that for an answer, but she'd hoped...

Robyn raised her chin, eyes flashing pain and anger. "If not Nick, then some other guy. It can't be that hard to find a willing man. Right?"

No, not hard. Pretty damned easy, in fact—just equally dangerous. Jumping directly into the sack with a stranger, out of anger and spite... Cassie grimaced. Setting her sights on a likely, harmless, *specific* temporary man was one thing. Fishing indiscriminately for a one-night stand just had disaster written all over it.

Cassie tried to sound reasonable. "No, it wouldn't be hard at all. But I don't want you to get hurt again. I mean, you're angry now. And you have a right to be angry—I'd be ticked if you weren't. But don't you think you should wait to cool down before you try something like this? I'd hate for you to regret—"

"No. I think it would be very unwise for me to sit on all these *histrionics*. Just this once, I want to make them work *for* me instead of *against* me."

Cassie considered, then spoke slow and thoughtfully. "That does make an odd sort of sense, I'll give you that." And maybe, once Robyn had seen some of her prospects or had a little time to cool off, she'd think better of it on her own. She wasn't an idiot. "So, let's go out, then."

"Good. Bars. A friend told me about a nightclub just down the street. She says it's an excellent place to meet guys."

"Sounds great." *Just great.*

"THIS WAS YOUR IDEA." Cassie gazed around the neon-flavored dance club. Gyrating bodies, tainted smoke and angry, throbbing music. One would have to be well and truly drunk to appreciate this as anything but a sleazy meat market for desperate singles and delinquent minors.

"I know, I know." Robyn glanced around, obviously agitated and annoyed. "I just thought—"

Cassie gave her a wry look. "No, you didn't. You were pissed and this was fast and easy."

"But totally ineffective."

"For your purposes, definitely." Cassie glanced around the bar. True, there were a lot of women here destined to get laid this evening, but she'd bet the majority would be disappointed by the experience.

Not a sober or normal man in the place, except—and these were only mild possibilities—the bartender and the bouncer.

"So do you have a better idea?" Robyn gave her a challenging look. Honestly, Cassie rejoiced at the light of battle in her friend's eyes, but this kind of follow-through was more than alarming. Robyn needed time to cool down before she got herself into some serious trouble.

So, think tame and talk. Less body contact than dance clubs. "Well...we could walk down the street to that sports bar," Cassie offered. "I'm sure there's a game on TV that's monopolizing everyone's attention, but at least you don't risk your shoes." Cassie glanced in the corner at one guy—possibly underaged?—who'd failed to take his illness as far as the men's room. Yuck.

"Either way, this is disgusting, Robyn." Cassie gave her a completely sober look. "You are not desperate. Impatient, sure, but *not* desperate."

At Robyn's disappointed frown, but agreeable shrug, Cassie relaxed a little. True, Robyn wasn't quite herself tonight, but the last thing she needed was for this, her first post-breakup venture back into the singles world, to end in complete failure. Perhaps a little carousing among friends would be sufficient to take the edge off the hurt Alex had inflicted. *Small-minded histrionics, my left butt cheek. Ugh. Alex, you insensitive ass, this is all your fault.*

"Okay, you're right. I need a little more dignity than this." Robyn sighed. "Let's try that sports bar, then."

They wove through a weaving crowd and out the door to inhale fresh air.

"Sorry about that." Robyn wrinkled her nose. "It really was awful, wasn't it."

"No harm done."

Robyn looked angry and dejected for a moment, before brightening. "Hey. A sports bar would be packed with men, right? Especially on a Saturday night." Robyn's eyes began to glitter, though Cassie suspected at least some of the sparkle was due to an onslaught of nerves. Sanity could be just around the corner. "Maybe I'll find a decent guy there."

"Could be."

The sports bar was indeed packed with men—men who couldn't take their eyes or minds off the massive television screens occupying two walls. Smaller sets blared down at them from corner shelves near the ceiling and around the bar. Beer and ball dominated the place; women were generally suspect. This was a serious sports bar.

A sharp crack rang out as bat met ball and the crowd went wild. Grown men stood on their chairs and whooped, fists raised to the ceiling and unattended beers splashing over mug rims.

Robyn gazed around, inspired. "Look. Just look at them. All that energy." She fixed a feverish smile on Cassie. "I want it focused on me. At least one set of energy and eyes. What do you think? *Sports.* What do you know about baseball?"

Cassie shrugged cautiously. "Enough to fake it occasionally in polite conversation? I don't know. You hit the ball and run the bases to score. That's really all there is to it. Leave it to grown men to turn hitting a ball with a stick into a near-religious obsession."

"*Yes!* I want to be a man's obsession. I always played second fiddle to Alex's *talent.* It's my turn now. I want to be first fiddle. Number one. An infatuation. That's *it.*

I want to be some *hot guy's infatuation*. Doesn't that sound lovely?"

Although jittery with nerves and excitement, Robyn had still managed to nail exactly what it was that every woman wanted from a romantic relationship. To be the recipient of some special man's exclusive adoration. Cassie nodded reluctantly. "Yeah. It really does sound good. Although, I'd bet something that strong and immediate would cool off quickly."

Robyn raised an eyebrow. "But probably on both sides, right? So no one's devastated. Isn't that what a satisfying fling's all about?"

"Yes. *Exactly* right."

"So how do we—"

"Hey, ladies. Lookin' hot to-*night*." Passing them, a guy tipped his ball cap and winked at them before a buddy claimed his attention.

Cassie glanced up, surprised, then happened to catch the sounds and sights of a commercial on TV. Ah. That explained it. The sports-obsessed flirted during commercial breaks. She grinned ruefully and shook her head. Even if Robyn found a guy she liked in this place, she'd still wind up playing second fiddle, only this time to a sports fetish.

Still, Robyn's flattered smile—and the woman was in serious need of flattery—made Cassie want to plant a wet one on the flirtatious guy's cheek. Until the female next to the flirty guy glared at them and reclaimed his arm.

Cassie shrugged, but saw Robyn looked a little unnerved. This wasn't her usual scene anymore. The woman was definitely experiencing growing pains. But at least the get-laid mania seemed to have passed for the moment. Sanity at last. Still, now was not the time to let Robyn scoot on home with her tail between her legs. She'd never emerge again if Cassie let her do that.

"Hey, why don't we find a table?" Cassie glanced around. "Better yet, you find us a table and I'll grab us some beers."

"Deal." Robyn looked relieved at having a task to perform.

"God, Robyn, *relax*, will you? They're not going to bite unless you ask them to." Cassie gave her a toothy grin.

"Dork." But Robyn was looking more like Robyn again.

Cassie raised her eyebrows for emphasis. "No corner tables, either. We're not hiding tonight, remember?"

"Right. You're right." As Robyn cut to the back, looking for an open table in a highly visible area, Cassie steeled herself and started weaving through the bodies-thick circumference of the bar. When she finally made it through, she managed to squeeze sideways between two sets of shoulders. She breathlessly requested two pints of whatever was on tap.

"Cassie?"

She glanced to her right, both delighted and panicked to encounter a set of sexy brown eyes so close to her own. "Nick. I—"

"Budweiser, Michelob, Bud Light, Mich Light..." the bartender recited in a bored voice, gaze still riveted to the television screen.

"Mich's great. Thanks. Oh, make one of those a Mich *Light,* please." She returned her attention to Nick.

"You're here with someone." He gave her a speculative look.

"Robyn."

"Ah," he murmured, leaning closer. "Not a date, then."

She smiled wryly. "No. Although..."

She gave him a speculative look of her own.

"Yes?" He dipped his head, his tone low and intimate.

"Robyn's finding us a table. She could probably use some help...."

He regarded her shrewdly. "I know what you're doing."

"What?"

He grinned. "You have beautiful eyes, but they just can't pull off that innocent look you're trying for."

She continued to bluff for a moment, but then, resigned and disgruntled, dropped the pose with a shrug. "I know. Never worked on my mom, either."

He laughed. "I'll bet. With looks like that, you must have given her fits as a kid."

"No, I didn't." She glanced up in surprise. "I was actually a well-behaved kid."

"Really." He leaned an elbow on the bar to turn and face her squarely. "Do tell."

"Not much to tell." She shrugged, glanced at the bartender, who looked occupied still, then back to Nick. "It was just the two of us, so me screwing up wasn't something either one of us could live with. We were close and careful to keep it that way. Probably because we knew each other was all we had to lose." She gave a self-deprecating laugh. "Yep. Me and Mom against the world. Evil-doers and bill collectors beware."

His grin faded to a curious smile. "I didn't know."

She shrugged. "How could you? We didn't know each other before without a beer in our hands." She grinned when the bartender brought her one of the beers she'd ordered. "Still don't." She opened her purse, but Nick nudged her wallet aside and paid for the drinks himself.

"Thanks." She smiled.

"Don't mention it."

"So...would you like to join us?" She raised her chin, searching once again for the bartender. Blessed, apparently, with sharp peripheral vision since his focus never left the television screen, the bartender held up a hand for patience. She turned back to Nick. "I'm still waiting on that second beer, but Robyn might have trouble getting us a table. Think you could help her out?"

He gave her a completely knowing look. "You're doing it again."

She blinked, briefly attempted innocence, then traded it in for a challenging smile. "Yeah, so? Want to sit with us or not?"

"Sure. But I can wait with you for the beer—"

"Please? Help Robyn? She's feeling a little out of place here. It would mean a lot to her."

He seemed to waver.

"Please?"

"See now, that eyelash-batting stuff is more your

style. Eloquent and effective." He nodded approvingly. "A guy can tell you're really making fun of him, but he's entertained enough not to care. Very nice."

That surprised a laugh out of her. "Thanks. I think."

He gave her a narrow-eyed look, softened by a rueful quirk of his lips. Then, with obvious reluctance, he turned to go find Robyn and the table.

Ignoring the patter of a fickle heart—Nick had lost not one iota of charm—Cassie tried to focus on something besides the image of Nick's sexy eyes, burned indelibly onto her field of vision. If anything, a few years had only honed the man's appeal.

She shook her head and forced the image away. Realizing the bartender was still enraptured with whatever play was on television, she counseled herself to patience. After all, it wouldn't hurt to give Robyn and Nick some time alone together. Wouldn't hurt at all.

Well, maybe just a little.

She frowned and shook it off. Nick was hot and charming, so of course it would still affect her. She was female and, like every female, she was at a certain hormonal disadvantage around handsome-rascal types. But she was also smart enough to realize it and to get over it. Right now, she should concentrate only on Nick's effect on Robyn. Charm like his should be sufficient to distract even heartbroken Robyn from her moody ex, her anger and her nerves.

Cassie winced. By now, Robyn had probably caved completely to nervousness. Cassie wouldn't be surprised to find Robyn had left the bar altogether.

"Here ya go." Bartender slid the second beer in front

of her and Cassie smiled her thanks. As she was turning to go, her gaze already scanning the bar for a familiar brunette, a cheerful voice stopped her.

"Hey, Cass." Robyn bumped her arm and accepted the beer Cassie handed her.

"Hey, yourself." Cassie smiled. Robyn seemed to have so far avoided nervous breakdown. "Couldn't find a table?"

"Lots of tables in back. But you took too long, so I came to find you." She gave Cassie a happy, carefree smile.

Too happy and too carefree. Cassie looked closer and immediately recognized the dilated pupils for the alcohol inspiration that they were. She also noted the newly acquired baseball cap settled sideways on Robyn's dark curls. "Robyn. You made friends."

Robyn giggled, confirming Cassie's suspicion. "Yep. The cutest one gave me the cap. And the tequila. Well, *they* actually suggested the tequila shots, but I did agree to the bet. Sort of a winner takes all deal."

"They? And the bet—"

"My new friends, remember? Names... Tim, I think. And Dan?" She shrugged. "We bet shots on the last batter is all. I lost. But I think they had insider information. I should have made them drink, too."

"Ah. It's all making scary sense now. So did you happen to see Nick on your way up here?"

"Nick? Nope. No sign of him. He's here?"

"He's looking for you and the table you're not saving for us."

Robyn giggled. "Well, we're not there to find."

"I see that." Cassie grinned ruefully. "Oh, well. He's a big boy. Maybe he'll think of checking back here for you."

"Maybe." Robyn sounded entirely too cheerful.

"Tequila, huh?" Not good. Too late now, but not good. At social functions, Robyn usually nursed a single drink all night, for show and for something to do with her hands. The woman was not a drinker. Concerned, Cassie discreetly slid the beer away from Robyn, who didn't seem to miss it.

"Yep. Good stuff. Speaking of good stuff." Robyn waggled her eyebrows. "Remember when I ran into Chad the other day? Well, once he got over his mile-high-club trauma, he had all kinds of tales to tell about our stud Nick."

"I'll bet." Cassie felt less than cheerful at the thought.

"Let's just say the man gets around and leave it at that."

Cassie grimaced. Words to remember.

As Cassie pondered fruitlessly, two guys squeezed in beside Robyn, identical smiles on their faces. Robyn had found twins? Cassie couldn't help a chuckle. Attractive twins enraptured with a single on the make; it was every guy's dream and here ultrafeminine *Robyn* had found it. What a kick.

Not that Robyn was the type, but hey, a woman could appreciate twisted irony on occasion.

Innocently pleased, Robyn looped an arm around each man's neck. "Well, hi, guys. Here's the friend I told you about. Isn't she cute? I told you she was cute."

Cassie groaned inwardly, but just laughed at the two

guys' assurances that she was indeed more attractive than a junkyard dog.

Robyn giggled. "So whatcha watchin'?" She focused on one of many televisions. "Oh, baseball. Cardinals. I remember. Happy guys?" She smiled and glanced at her twins, who seemed thrilled at the attention.

"Yeah. Season just opened." Tim—or was it Dan?—offered the information helpfully, his gaze never leaving Robyn's pretty, glassy-eyed face.

Cassie muffled another chuckle. Robyn had always been highly effective with the opposite sex, but it was entirely unconscious. And usually entertaining.

*Usually.* But Robyn's tequila seemed to be catching up with her, more and more every moment.

"Mmm. I like baseball." Robyn continued watching, bumping gently against one of the guys. "Much better than football." She turned to one of the twins. "Do you like football?"

He smiled at her. "I love football."

Robyn smiled back in sloppy affection, but then frowned at a sudden thought and wrinkled her nose. "Oh, but it's the Rams now, isn't it? The Cardinals left? What a bummer." She sighed and shook her head, then continued in a tequila-induced bellow. "You know, it's such a shame that the football Cardinals left St. Louis. Their uniforms were so much prettier than those dull blue ones we had to watch all winter."

Voices died down to a low roar. Heads swiveled, eyes refocused. Twins cautiously receded into the background. An angry murmuring began.

"What?" Robyn looked sincerely confused and gazed

in a generalized manner around the bar. "*What?* I was just making conversation. Oh, come on. Admit it. That's got to be one of the most *butt-ugly* shades of blue you've ever seen. Ugh. The other guys had that crisp red-and-white combination—and it coordinated so well with the baseball team. Cardinals, Cardinals." She shook her head sorrowfully. "We really had a nice thing going. Now it's all ruined."

"Robyn," Cassie murmured urgently. "Shut. Up."

"Why? I'm just talking about uniforms."

Painfully aware of several "butt-ugly" blue jerseys displayed with pride on the bar's walls, Cassie ducked slightly. She lowered her voice to a choked-sounding whisper. "Robyn, please. These are not normal people. They are sports fans. And you are committing sacrilege."

Robyn huffed. "Spoilsports. Can't take a little criticism. Honestly." She tipped her chin high and spoke in an exaggerated snarl. "Some armchair athletes just have no fashion sense." She chortled at her own wit.

Cassie cringed. Some observations were hysterical when shared over drinks among like-minded female friends. These same witticisms, however, were usually best left unspoken in a sports bar full of, well, *armchair athletes*. Maybe some of the guys looked fit enough to be real athletes. She discreetly scanned the area, noting the distinct lack of welcome in formerly intrigued faces. Perhaps not this crowd. They seemed a little...defensive. Less than amenable.

"Wow, Robyn. Look at the time, will you? We'd better be going. We have an early, er, *thing* to do. Remember? The thing?"

"There's a thing? A work thing?" Robyn looked disgruntled. "You didn't tell me there was a thing. Isn't tomorrow Sunday?"

"Um, sure." Cassie thought quickly, improvised. "This is an unusual thing. Last-minute type." *Fictional type.*

"Oh." Robyn pouted but seemed to accept. "You're not supposed to let me near alcohol on the night before we have a thing. Remember?" A precaution from their college days, and one that certainly bore remembering.

"I do now. Come on, lush. Let's get you home." Cassie snagged Robyn's arm, tossed a conciliatory smile and huge tip at the hostile bartender, and slid off her bar stool. "I swear I don't know anyone else who can get drunk on a shot of tequila."

Robyn snickered. "I had three. One, two, *three*."

"Oh, no."

"Ye-up." Robyn leaned against Cassie, gave her a sleepy smile, then sagged completely.

Cassie staggered under the sudden weight and bumped against a bar stool, which toppled loudly. "Well. So much for dignity." She glanced around, looking for a stable place to prop Robyn while she picked up the stool—

"Need some help?"

She glanced up, way up, into chocolate-brown eyes sparkling with wicked amusement. And nearly dropped Robyn.

Help? Oh, yeah. She needed help in a bad, bad way.

# _____Step 5_____

_Blackmail or Barter_
_Under duress, we admit to our personal shortcomings._

CASSIE GLANCED between Nick's laughing eyes and
Robyn's closed ones and groaned inwardly. Fate was a
fickle woman and Cassie was obviously on her black-
list. The situation was ludicrous. Well, so much for any
matchmaking attempts, at least for this evening. This
evening she would devote to damage control.

"Robyn...believe it or not...is almost laughably sensitive to alcohol."

"Mmm. I can see that." After righting the stool while
manfully ignoring the jeering males around them, Nick
turned back to Cassie.

"No, really. It's more than just being a lightweight. So
she usually sticks to cola or a single, really weak drink.
But I think she was nervous tonight."

Nick's grin twisted slightly with empathy. "False
courage?"

"Yeah."

"Is she going to be okay? Do we need to take her to an
emergency room?"

Cassie patted Robyn's cheek, watched her friend give
her a bleary but still-wide-eyed smile, and glanced back

to Nick. "I think she'll be okay. Sick as a dog in a little while, but I saw her worse than this in college a few times." She gave a rueful grin. "She'll be absolutely mortified tomorrow, though. Especially if I tell her about the uniform crack." She glanced around, relieved to see that the guys had already dismissed her and Robyn as beneath their notice.

Nick grinned.

Cassie chuckled. "Absolutely mortified. And I'm going to have to play nice. Totally unfair." She shook her head. "But I can't pick on her when she's down. Poor Robyn here just broke up with her boyfriend and she's not used to all this socializing stuff anymore. It'd be easy for anyone to screw up."

"I know how that goes." He murmured it while helping Cassie lever Robyn to an upright position.

Cassie gave him a disbelieving look before stumbling and finally shrugging Robyn's arm over her shoulder. "Right. Like you'd know anything about discomfort with the social scene. Or getting over a long-term relationship."

He grinned. "Well, I'll admit the latter's a bit outside my experience. But as for the social scene," he shrugged, "with work and all, I really haven't had much free time until lately. Work, eat, sleep. I'm taking more time for myself now that things are going more smoothly, but things have changed. The whole bar scene that was second nature just a few short years ago, just isn't as comfortable as it once was."

Cassie gave him a thoughtful look. "Okay. I can buy that. Sort of." No doubt every woman on the "scene" would welcome him back with open arms, though, and he'd be feeling more at home before he knew it.

"So, shall we?" He glanced meaningfully toward Robyn and nodded toward the exit.

"Yes, please." Cassie murmured it with feeling, then grunted as she shifted Robyn's weight and began maneuvering her toward the door.

Nick carefully held Robyn's other arm, and between them, they managed to goose-walk her out into the fresh night air. The quiet was almost deafening after the noisy bar.

"Where's your car?" Nick glanced around.

Cassie grimaced. "At my apartment? We walked."

"Well, then...Nick Ranger, at your service." He bobbed a head, eliciting a rueful grin from her. "My Jeep's right over here."

"Thank you." She flashed him a heartfelt glance. As slender as Robyn was, she was also quite tall. Not a lightweight in every respect. Especially as deadweight. Robyn's lips parted and a soft snurkle emerged. Cassie winced for her.

Nick chuckled and helped Cassie tote her friend to his Jeep and gently ease her into the back seat. Once all limbs were accounted for and arranged, Nick eased the door shut and opened the passenger one for Cassie.

"Oh, but..." She glanced between Nick and Robyn. Alone together in a car would have been great. Unfortunately, one of the parties was passed out. And needed a baby-sitter.

Nick raised a questioning eyebrow, but his eyes were knowing. Again. That could get to be annoying.

"Thank you." Just to be contrary, she gracefully slid into the car and raised an imperious eyebrow to let him know he could close the door for her.

Chuckling, he did so. As he rounded the car, she unbent from her dignity enough to unlock his door for him.

"So, where to?"

Cassie wrinkled her nose. "My place would be best. Her car's still there."

"My pleasure."

Nick dropped over two blocks and down a street before slowing to a stop in front of Cassie's apartment building. Flipping on his hazards, he rounded the vehicle again and helped tug Robyn out of it.

"Um, I think I can take it from here...."

"Don't be an idiot, Cass. I promise not to take advantage of you or your friend. I'm just trying to help, okay?"

"I know. And I appreciate it."

"Let's go."

Together, they maneuvered Robyn up the stairs and into Cassie's second-floor apartment, where they lowered her onto the couch.

Cassie turned back to Nick. "Sorry we cut your evening short. I appreciate the help." She glanced back at the couch before turning a wry grin on Nick. "And so would Robyn if she were conscious."

Nick laughed. "No doubt."

"So, um..."

He cocked his head, waiting, but she just waved a hand awkwardly. Now that they were inside the apartment, leaving even city street noises behind them, the place was silent as a tomb. Unnerving.

When she didn't continue, he spoke quietly into the silence. "So, were you serious? About owing me one?"

She gave him a wary look. "I...yes. Within reason."

"Within reason." He scratched his chin, eyes twinkling. He knew what she was thinking. She could see it there in that devilish grin he was holding back, just barely.

She narrowed her eyes at him, verbal lash at the ready.

"How about if we trade for a few Web site lessons? I mean, I still want you to build my site, but once that's done...I could probably maintain it myself, right?"

She blinked, deflated and almost disappointed that he didn't request sexual recompense. Okay, no almost about it, not that she'd admit anything of the sort to him, thanks. "Lessons?"

"Well, yeah. Just how to make changes or update? I'd still have you do the design stuff and major changes when we needed it, but if I just wanted to fiddle with schedules or rates...isn't that something I could do myself?"

"Sure. Sure." She nodded, thinking. Maybe she could use this. To Robyn's advantage. She raised her chin and spoke more forcefully. "That sounds great, actually. Web site lessons."

He smiled. "Good. When do we start?"

Ten nearly platonic minutes later—the only exception being Cassie's fantasies—they'd finalized arrangements for the first "tutoring" session and Nick had made a polite exit. Somehow, Cassie thought Nick had more in mind than Web site building for these sessions, but that was just fine with her.

Because she had a little something extra in mind, too. She gazed thoughtfully at Robyn's unconscious form.

Matchmaking.

"OH. GOD. I feel like absolute hell." Robyn groaned and buried her face under the pillow again.

"Bucket? You need a bucket." Cassie nimbly snatched up a wastepaper basket and placed it within heaving distance of Robyn's head.

"No. I think I'm finally done with that." Robyn turned her head so Cassie could see her pale face sandwiched between pillow and cushion.

Pale but not green. "Thank God." Relieved, Cassie sat carefully on the edge of the couch in front of her friend. It had been a long night. "Oh, Robyn. Why?"

Robyn groaned. "I'm sorry. I know, I know. It was stupid to drink. It always messes me up and I know it. I was just nervous and there were these two guys who seemed interested and it felt good. And they suggested the bet...and I guess I just wanted to play along, you know? Jump right into the singles scene without the old, awkward explanations about teetotaling and goody-goodies."

Cassie gave her a crooked grin. "I know. But the alternative's not so great, either."

Robyn just mumbled agreement.

"It'll be easier next time...." Cassie offered tentatively.

Robyn opened an eye. "Next time? Oh, I think I'm done now."

"You're giving up, then? So we should just get you a pretty little cat and a rocker so you can smoke cigars and wail limericks into the sunset?" Cassie batted taunting eyelashes at her friend. There was a time to coddle and a time to bully.

Robyn managed to slit both bloodshot eyes open and glare at her friend before closing them. "This is not comforting me."

"Of course it's not. You don't want to give up and you know it. That's just the hangover speaking."

"No, it's not."

"Oh. I'm sorry." Cassie feigned sympathy. "So we really are going to let Alex win? Maybe you're going to go crawling back to him so you can apologize for...some small-minded histrionics?" Way low and Cassie knew it. But the occasional big guns were required.

Robyn groaned low into the pillow, but it built into a moderate roar until she threw the pillow at Cassie and clumsily maneuvered herself into a sitting position. The better for glaring at her best friend. "That's cheating."

"All's fair..."

"That's worse."

"Yeah, I know." Cassie sprawled happily on the floor. Robyn was back. "I got you a date, though."

"A date? Not the twins."

Cassie chuckled. "No, not the twins. We owe Nick some Web site maintenance lessons."

"Web site maintenance? But that's your specialty.

And I'd bet he's expecting that you'll play teacher, not me."

"Not necessarily. I only promised him lessons. And the stuff's basic enough that you can teach it as well as I can. Part of the two-fer deal, remember?"

Robyn groaned. "You're shameless."

"Just determined. This could actually work if you give it a chance."

Robyn shook her head. "Fine. Whatever. So why do we owe him this? You don't usually offer that kind of thing with the standard package."

"It's payback for chauffeur services. He drove us here last night while you were incapacitated."

Robyn stared, her face going even paler. "You mean, Nick saw me like that? And now I have a date with him? Do you *hate* me, Cassie?"

Cassie waved a hand. "It's okay. I did damage control for you. I think it might even work in your favor. Proof that you're not a desperate barfly."

"Just a sloppy boozer."

Cassie chuckled. "You can bet Nick's had his share. And he understood. It's okay. And you didn't do anything disgusting in front of him. Well, almost...."

"What?" Robyn shrieked, then held her head in pain.

Cassie gave her a wicked look. "Let's just say it's a darn good thing the guy wasn't wearing butt-ugly blue."

"Butt-ugly..." Robyn looked blank for a moment before squeezing her eyes shut and moaning. "Oh, God. It was real?"

"Oooooh, yeah." Cassie grinned. "But I promise not to tell you more if you agree to the date with Nick."

"Just answer this first. Did I say all that in front of him?"

"I don't think so..."

"Well, okay then. I'll do the Web site lessons. So, now that you have me where you want me, what was the disgusting thing you didn't tell me?"

"Nothing. Just consider it payback for nursing duty." She grinned and fielded the pillow Robyn tossed at her. "You're meeting him here a week from Tuesday. Six-thirty."

"YOU WANT TO GO OUT? Really? After what happened last weekend?" Cassie stared at the phone before holding it to her ear again.

Cassie had thought Robyn would protest any and all socializing for weeks after the sports bar humiliation. In fact, Cassie had already written off this weekend as lost and had resolved to kidnapping Robyn in time for the Tuesday night Web site lesson with Nick. But no. It was just Saturday night, after a mere week's worth of re-criminations and self-lashings, and here was Robyn calling, ready to party. "You're kidding me. God, Robyn, I thought I was going to have to blackmail you to get you to go out again."

"You already did that." Robyn spoke with wry annoyance.

Cassie grinned briefly. "Yeah. Brilliant, wasn't it?"

"Brilliant all right, darling. But that's Tuesday. Three whole days away. I don't want to waste the rest of the weekend on hopes for a Tuesday night Web design lesson." Robyn sounded downright perky. Volatile. Again? No one recovered from a butt-ugly-blue incident plus hangover with this much enthusiasm. Unless bribed, medicated or provoked.

Cassie considered, then closed her eyes. She was betting on provoked. "Alex. Again."

"There was a 2:00 in the a.m. phone message from the slime on my voice mail. Apparently he was *in the mood* last night."

"Oh. Dead man."

"If I'd been here to take the call, he might have been. After everything that's happened, he actually thinks I'm ready to hop into the sack just because for him all systems are go? The man can dream. I might be a sexually frustrated woman, but I hope I have more pride than that. No, if I'd been here, his ears would have been burning by the time I hung up that phone."

"But even better...you were out?" Cassie pondered the situation. Alex, despite himself, was helping Cassie's cause immensely. Silly, silly man.

"Exactly. He doesn't need to know I was just getting some work done at the coffeehouse. I want him to think I was out on the town. Maybe with another guy even. And I intend to be *out* again tonight. He and his right hand can just dream, for all I care."

"Alex is right-handed? I thought for sure he'd be a lefty. Aren't most artists left-handed? Or is that just with regard to their art. Not...other stuff." She tried for deadpan. It worked.

Robyn sputtered, then laughed. "God, Cassie, you're

too much. How should I know how or what, oh, never mind. The point is, he's not having *me*."

"Good girl. So what's the plan this time?"

"Well, a friend of mine called and they need two more females for this great new…"

# _____Step 6_____

_Speed Dating_
_We confront a catalog of our defects...in five minutes or less._

SO THIS WAS SPEED DATING. The dating panacea for today's busy, ambitious single. Cassie glanced around the
restaurant. Robyn's friend, who owned a matchmaking
service and had found herself short two women at the
last minute, had invited Robyn and Cassie to partici-
pate gratis. Robyn was thrilled, Cassie less so.

Currently the participants were congregating in the
back room of a restaurant and fourteen singles—seven
men and seven women—were participating in a surreal, adult version of musical chairs.

Every five minutes, at the event coordinator's call, the
men would all rise from their seats and shift one chair
to the right, with the end man rounding to a chair at the
farthest left of the column of tables. This way, each single was ensured an equal opportunity at each single of
the opposite sex. And the women didn't have to move,
which Cassie counted as a plus. Her shoes, while utterly
adorable, were borrowed and utterly killing her.

"So what do you do for a living?" The blonde, Alan,
spoke quietly and quickly. He was clean-cut, attractive

in a bland, fading sort of way, and he obviously had a checklist of questions. This was the first.

"I'm a Web designer. It's—"

"I know what it is." He gave her a brusque smile. "And what is your five-year plan? Does it include family and a career or do you plan to devote yourself to one or the other exclusively?"

Cassie blinked. "Well, I honestly hadn't thought—"

He nodded, mentally checking off a box, she could see.

"What are your political leanings? Conservative, liberal?"

"Well, I tend to ride the fence. An independent, but not of the Independent Party...."

*Check.*

"What are your hobbies? How much time do you devote to each?"

Cassie blinked. Time? As in *free* time? What the hell was that, anyway? "My friends? My business? I belong to a gym." Not that she actually *used* it yet...

"You work out." He nodded approvingly.

Great. Thanks to a near lie, she'd finally made the cut. How thrilling. Arrogant ass.

"So what about you?" Cassie turned it back on him. "What's your career plan?"

He smiled complacently. "I'm in marketing, with a direct line to an upper management position."

"And when can you hope to attain that position?"

He paused, but only briefly. "It's in my five-year plan."

"Will you be able to support twelve children on your

income?" She smiled sweetly. "It's very important to me."

"Twelve..."

As Alan stammered in dismay, the coordinator called time.

"Oh, Alan, thank you. I'm definitely putting you on my list of must-see-agains." She oozed goodwill and acquisitiveness, finally gaining the appalled look she dearly coveted. "I want to work overseas, too, so I hope your child-rearing skills are excellent."

With a cheery wave, Cassie watched him hastily slide one chair to his right. Good riddance.

Another man slid into the vacated seat across from her. "Hi. I'm Cassie."

"Perry. Nice to meet you. So what do you do...?"

And so it continued, one man after the other, with the name tags changing and the questions and facial expressions varying only slightly. Robyn had called it speed dating for the on-the-go single. Cassie thought a better term would be assembly-line dating for the efficiently acquisitive. Or: terrifying.

"So, is this what you thought it would be?" Cassie murmured the question to Robyn as they waved their farewells.

"Well. We met a lot of guys." Robyn murmured it back, sounding less than confident.

"Yes. Seven. I met seven. You met seven. Everyone who attended met seven representatives of the opposite sex. The egalitarian approach to dating. Do you suppose they use that in their advertising?"

"Cass." Robyn shushed her, discreetly scanning for eavesdroppers.

"Ugh. I think I feel dirty."

Robyn choked. "Cut it out."

"Come on. It was like interviewing for a job. Interviewing for a job that could very possibly involve sex at some later point...get it? We're back to the old prostitution proposition." Snickering, Cassie turned to lead the way out and ran smack into something tall and hard. Something familiar.

"Well, nice to see you again, too." Nick grinned down at her.

She frowned up at him. "Why are you here?"

He shrugged in mock apology. "It wasn't expressly forbidden, so I thought I could enter the restaurant and have dinner with the rest of the patrons. They serve food here and I was hungry." He ended on a plaintive note that had Cassie laughing reluctantly despite her growing embarrassment.

"So, you were here on...an interview?"

Cassie groaned. *Might as well get it over with.* "You did hear."

"The prostitution proposition? Well, I'll admit to some curiosity. So who's the prostitute and who's the proposition?" He waggled eyebrows to take the sting out of his words. The guy was turning her flub into a joke so she didn't die of embarrassment. How sweet was that?

But he wasn't supposed to be sweet—at least, not to her. "Robyn." She glanced to her side.

Robyn was giving her a wry look. "Why do I feel like a security blanket?"

Nick laughed.

Cassie raised her nose and gave them both a superior look through a still-embarrassed flush. "So that's what a girl gets for trying to be polite. I was just trying to be conversationally inclusive. Avoid hurt feelings. Not offend. And besides, Robyn drove, so I'm at her mercy, transportationally speaking." There, take that, baby.

"And now Robyn goes bye-bye." Robyn smiled slyly, then pivoted and strode out of the restaurant.

"Hey." When Cassie made to go after her, Nick murmured, "Chicken."

Cassie spun back. *"Chicken? She's my ride."* You're steak. I'm starving. Just a logical progression...

"I have a car—and a table. And I was just getting ready to order dessert. Want to split one with me? Please?" He tried to look pathetic. Cassie was quite certain that was his intent. "I'd even let you order one of your own if you want."

She narrowed her eyes, trying not to smile at the rascal. "You know, you have gorgeous eyes, but they don't quite carry off that poor-little-me look you're trying for."

He laughed, eyes glittering appreciatively as she volleyed his own words from the sports bar back at him.

Damn, but the man was hot when he laughed. "Now that devilish appeal..." She shook her head, trying desperately to keep a wistful note out of her voice. "Yeah, that'll take you places."

"Good. Dessert?"

She wavered. Nick's dark chocolate eyes, plus dessert. Mercy?

"They make an excellent version of Death by Chocolate here." He raised an eyebrow, coaxing. "Brownie, mousse, chocolate sauce, dark chocolate shavings, nuts...?"

What was a girl to do? "Sure, okay. Dessert sounds great." Besides, he was probably here with his partners, so it didn't have to be a cozy little chat for two. She could do this. And maybe a good dose of chocolate would help her feel better about sacrificing to dark chocolate eyes.

She followed him back to his—empty?—table. "You're here alone?"

He shrugged. "I had to work today and it was a long one. I just wanted to unwind. Sometimes I like to eat out alone." He smiled. "Makes for great people watching."

Cassie glanced around, saw a few sets of feminine eyes trained on Nick, and nodded knowingly. No doubt he arrived alone and left with company. Much like this evening...?

"So you had to work today. For the Drummonds?"

He laughed. "No, not for the Drummonds. I should have a decent month or two before facing them again."

"A respite. Too bad one of them doesn't get airsick. You could be spared future spectacles."

He shook his head, looking pained. "I'm going to have to figure something out."

A waitress politely interrupted them and they both quickly gave their orders.

After the woman had left, Cassie gave Nick an inquiring look. "So is this couple old, as in *decrepit*, or just mature and healthy?"

"Why?" He gave her an amused, cautious look.

She shrugged. "Well, you could do loop-de-loops in the plane or feed them laxatives or something like that. But not if they're going to keel over and die on you."

He laughed. "You are vicious."

"Maybe. But I don't think it's right for them to put you in the position you're in. They know exactly what they're doing. And they're getting off on it. I think that's worth a few loop-de-loops, Cowboy."

He grimaced. "A good point. However, the Drummonds were pretty decent to my parents at a time when they needed it. You could say we owe them."

She gave him a skeptical look. "How decent is decent? Decent enough to merit you tolerating the almost-mile-high club?"

He shrugged, looking torn. "Decent to my family when my folks were pretty desperate."

"How so?"

"Well, about seven or eight years ago, my dad got pretty sick. He was in and out of the hospital trying to find out what was wrong and he just kept getting worse. He had to quit his job and I tried to help out with money, but it got to the point where my folks were afraid they were going to have to sell their house to make ends meet."

"Seven or eight years ago...and then you left college." She gave him a surprised look. "That's why you left." Not partying. Family concerns and money.

"Well, yeah." He shrugged off the observation as

moot. "Anyway, what it all came down to was that the Drummonds gave my folks a sizable personal loan, based on faith alone. Just because they were friends. And it got them through."

"Wow. And how's your dad now?"

The waitress set their desserts in front of them and Cassie smiled a thank-you before turning an expectant gaze on Nick.

"Dad's fine now. The doctors figured out what it was, got him on some good medication and he's doing better now. He went back to work and my folks are back on their feet again. But if the Drummonds hadn't helped out—" He shrugged and scooped a bit of chocolate mousse.

"So you're saying diplomacy's required."

"That's about the size of it."

She frowned for a moment, chewing, then gestured with her fork. "You could get them train tickets. Or a train pass or whatever package deal they offer."

He laughed. "Whatever. My problem. So what were you and Robyn up to? I saw you two leave the back room with a group. Some big deal with clients?"

"I wish."

He looked crestfallen. "So you don't generally wine and dine all your clients? Damn. I was hoping to leave you with my tab."

She narrowed her eyes at him while he scooped up another spoonful of chocolatey dessert.

Chewing, he gave her a wicked look and a wink before continuing. "So what was it if not business? You sound less than thrilled about it."

"Oh, let me tell you." She shook her head, then wished she could take back the words.

"Please." When she hesitated, he tried a coaxing look. "Come on. What could it hurt?"

She made a face.

"Okay, let me guess, then. You're part of an underground, politically subversive group with plans to get your imaginary friend elected president?"

She choked on a mouthful of brownie. "Idiot."

"Maybe something simpler? An orgy?" He looked hopeful.

"Pervert."

"So there you go." He gestured widely and somehow philosophically. "The truth is obviously not nearly as outrageous as either of those and I pulled them out of my own twisted little mind. See? I can handle the truth. Lay it on me."

She gave up. "Ever heard of speed dating?"

He gave her a nonplussed look. "Sort of like skipping the bases and declaring an automatic home run?"

"Will you ever leave adolescence behind you? *No.* This is not about sex." She raised her eyebrows pointedly. "In fact, the experience would have been a lot less unsettling if it *had* been about sex. Or if it actually involved anything *remotely* related to natural attraction between the sexes. But no, this was cold and clinical."

"So what was its purpose then?"

She thought for a moment. "To decide, in five minutes or less, whether or not another person was your soul mate. Or at least, whether this person measured up to a specified checklist of characteristics desirable in a potential significant other."

"Ouch."

"Efficient, though, I'll give 'em that. I could tell in five minutes or less that I'd never date somebody with a checklist. I could never measure up—but I'd like to think they couldn't, either. At least not to what I'm looking for in a relationship. It was...romance for the romantically challenged."

"Socializing for the sexually apathetic?" he offered.

"Fast-food dating for the fashionably feckless?" she countered.

"Drive-thru service for the determined but dateless?"

She rolled her eyes but grinned. "I think you're getting the idea." She dug into more chocolate.

"Well, I am and I'm not. So, if you know what you don't want in a relationship...maybe you also know what you *do* want?"

"More or less." She was hedging and she knew it.

"Tell me the more part."

"You would ask that."

He grinned.

"Well...*I* don't know." She was flustered. "I mean, at the very least, I'd like to start with some attraction. I don't think that's too much to ask—that I start talking to a guy because I'm drawn to him."

"The way he looks?"

"Well...no. Yes. And no. I mean, it *is* the first thing you notice, right?"

"Right. Nothing wrong with that."

"I mean, maybe I'll like a guy's smile and something

a little extra in his expression or the look in his eyes. Or maybe we'll just really *get* each other's sense of humor. But you won't find any of that on a list of names attending a function. And if you're too busy marking off a checklist or asking stupid questions instead of concentrating on the person in the here and now...you'll never know. How could you know?"

"Cassie."

She glanced up, still lost in her logic. "What? You don't agree?"

"I agree." Setting down his fork, he took her hand. "I also like your smile. It's sexy and sassy and provoking. And the look in your eyes sometimes... Well, it drives me straight through the roof. Or knocks me flat on my ass." His hand tightened around hers before relaxing.

She stared, glad she was sitting. It saved her the trouble of falling. Flat on her ass.

His eyes darkened. "Like now, for example. Will you go out with me?"

"You're kidding, right?" She tried a sickly sounding laugh. "I mean, it's all part of that drive-thru dating for the feckless and determinedly apathetic and sexual..." She cringed, dropping her fork.

He smiled at her, his fingers caressing the back of her hand. "I was hoping we could skip the drive-thru and the feckless and the apathetic...but not the sexual, of course."

She swallowed. Hard.

"I mean, we did already agree that sexual attraction is just part of the whole process. Not the be-all and end-all, but certainly a beginning...."

To, very possibly, Cassie's own-be-all, end-all of relationships. Falling in love with Nick would be the height of stupidity. "Er, right, but..." She croaked the words, suddenly seeing the walls rising up on either side of her. Cornered. No, not yet. She could stop this foolishness before it was too late.

"But what?" He smiled at her, his thumb caressing a tiny circle on the back of her hand.

She tugged it free, staring at Nick and absently rubbing the tingling little circle. When his gaze dipped low, to her hands and their movements, Cassie snatched them under the table and gripped them tightly in her lap.

"Cassie?"

"I...can't, Nick." Oh, a girl shouldn't have to deny herself like this... "Really. I'm not playing games or..."

"Then why? We seem to have fun together no matter where we are. Right?"

"Well, yes, but—"

"So that means we really get each other's sense of humor. I know you make me laugh and, unless you're a hell of an actress, I think I've entertained you in the past, too."

She smiled at that. Not that Nick had any doubts, she knew. The man didn't lack for confidence.

"So why don't we go out? See where this thing leads?"

"I—"

"Heck, even your friends seem to like me. Robyn does."

*Robyn. Blind spots. Male addiction.*

*Matchmaking.*

"Right. I know. But...we can't date."

He gave her a direct look, demanding no less than the truth.

She sighed. "Look. I've really, really talked you up to Robyn. She knows I've been trying to set the two of you up."

He smiled. "Robyn looks smarter than that to me. She seems nice enough, but I think even she can see what's between you and me. Why fight it?"

"Well, *because.* I mean—" She floundered, avoiding the temporary man versus relationship man argument. It couldn't help but sound insulting and she really didn't want to do that. And that whole blind spot analogy was just too humiliating—and revealing. She'd settle for impersonal. Plus numbers. "Well, there's this business relationship between us. You're paying me to design your site."

She considered, then wryly included a more solid truth. "From friends and past experiences, I've discovered it's generally unwise to date a guy if money is changing hands."

His lips twitched. "The prostitution proposition?"

She laughed. "Sort of, but not really. It just seems to complicate matters that are already complicated."

"They don't have to be complicated. We date when we're social, we exchange money when we're professional."

"Ah. You want to compartmentalize. Did I ever mention that, for a techie, I'm really rotten at compartmentalizing? At the risk of appearing politically incorrect,

I'd like to suggest that it's a gender thing. I don't know a single female capable of compartmentalizing. Then again, I also don't know of a single male who's capable of true multitasking." She was babbling. She knew it. Could she help it? Of course not. *Help.*

He did. "Cassie." He leaned forward. "I think it would be a mistake not to—"

"Why, Nick Ranger, as I live and breathe." A tall—really tall—brunette stopped by the table and settled her hands on curvy hips.

Cassie blinked. Wavy hair, big boobs, bottleneck waist and she refused to even think about the penny-size—but necessarily *firm*—ass on the woman. Just a combination of curves that would no doubt leave every man slobbering foolishly in her wake. A knockout. Smiling at Nick. Just lovely.

"Shannon." Nick sat back and met the woman's gaze. "How's it going?"

"Oh, just great. I got that promotion I wanted, by the way."

"Congratulations." He smiled up at her, his eyes sincere.

"Yep. And now I get paid almost twice as much to do about half the amount of work." She gave him a contented little smile, lashes gently lowering to perfectly sculpted cheekbones. "Why, I have all kinds of money and time on my hands now. I'll have to find something useful to do with it all."

"Oh. Yeah." Nick blinked, his gaze swerving to Cassie. "Um, Shannon. This is Cassie. She...we knew each other in school. She's a Web designer. And she's building my Web site now."

Gosh, what an enthusiastic description. Cassie wanted to kill him. But what, after all, did she expect? Just because he was still catching his breath from asking Cassie out, he should forego a brand-new opportunity? Cassie was, after all, attempting to turn him down and he had to realize that.

"Oh, school friends. Isn't that nice?" Shannon smiled at Cassie, completely malice-free.

Cassie smiled back, less enthused.

"I met Nick after he left all that college stuff behind him," Shannon continued. "We had some good times, didn't we, Nick?"

"Yeah, we did." He smiled at her, caught Cassie's gaze, then spoke again. "But that was a while ago. Months."

Shannon tsked. "Not so long, Nick. Maybe a couple of months, but we were just so busy. Outside of work, it was hard to squeeze but an evening or two a month out of you." She smiled fondly. "But it was worth it. Cowboy." She shook her head. "You and that plane, Nicholas Ranger."

"Right." He cleared his throat. "It's a good business."

Shannon laughed outright. "Business. Sure. Just like that time you were flying back from Kansas City with important cargo for my dad and your plane's engine blew. You had to play glider." She laughed. "Some business decision. Why, I thought Jerry was going to blow a gasket just watching you. That thing sputtered back on just in time."

He closed his eyes, grinning ruefully. "If I'd had to land that plane on its belly...oh, man. Talk about damage and dollars. The freight for your dad's company, my poor plane... Yeah, that could have killed the business for sure."

Cassie gave him a shocked look, utterly speechless. Killed...the *business?* Hello? What about his idiotic hide? He could have killed himself taking a plane down like that. Especially one as dinky as the two he currently flew.

"Well, Nick, I see you're busy." The lovely Shannon gave Nick a wistful, teasing look. "Call me sometime. You have my number...." She waved a few fingers at Cassie and walked off to seat herself with a small group on the other side of the restaurant.

Cassie seethed. Forced herself to try *not* to seethe. But still she seethed. What gall. So maybe Cassie didn't intend to date Nick, but Miss Curvy Butt didn't know that. And yet she'd had the gall to issue Nick an open invitation that any idiot could interpret as a no-strings booty call. Had the woman no pride?

Cassie groaned inwardly. Then again, maybe the woman had all the pride and assurance she needed. No doubt Nick was more than ready to drop-kick Cassie back to her computer so he could get down and dirty with Shannon.

"Cassie?" Nick slid a hand across the table. "About that date?"

She forced a smile, albeit a toothy one. "Don't worry about it. We already knew this wasn't going anywhere."

"Maybe you did, but I didn't." He frowned at her. "Look, if this is about Shannon...she and I dated for a while, but it was never serious and I honestly haven't seen her in months."

Cassie held up both hands in an approximation of good will allowing free will. "Hey, your prerogative and not my business."

"Cass—"

She stood up, digging through her purse for enough cash to cover her portion. "Hey, why don't you flag the waiter down and ask for the check? I'll be right back. Ladies' room." She smiled, blindly tossed a few bills on the table and slipped away before he responded.

Deep breath in, deep breath out, deep breath in... She'd heard deep breaths were one of those emotional cure-alls. Feeling a little nervous? Deep breaths. Getting scared? Inhale, exhale. Feel the need to either jump a guy or beat him dead? Air in, air out.

Air in, air out.

Inhale, exhale.

"Idiots don't know what they're talking about." Cursing under her breath and still feeling volatile, Cassie took the ladies' room door on the fly, listening to it bang shut behind her. She yanked a paper towel out of the dispenser and ran cold water over it. After wringing it out, she blotted her temples, her neck, feeling the cool settle her nerves where the stupid breathing had not. She sighed in relief.

Then the door behind her swung open and a sky-scraper-heeled woman with sleek hair and clothes stepped in. She smiled at Cassie as she walked past and set her bag on a ledge above the sink to pull out a lipstick. She touched up, smacked her lips, puckered, then capped the lipstick once more before turning her gaze back on Cassie. "Oh, hi."

"Hi?"

The woman smiled. "You were sitting with Nick, right? I'm with Shannon."

*Goody.* Cassie just nodded.

The woman's smile widened. "It's funny."

Cassie raised an eyebrow, quite sure it wasn't going to be.

"You. Nick. Shannon. Me. Bet we could all tell some stories."

Nope, not going to be funny. "I'm not sure what you mean."

"Maybe a better grouping would have been you, me and Shannon." Her smile widened to display even, white teeth. "Why, we could compare notes. On Nick."

"Oooh. Classy. But I think I'll pass, thanks." Cassie just gave her a harmless smile and tossed the towel in the trash before leaving. She was really going to have to do something about these homicidal tendencies. They seemed to be getting worse, the target varying.

On that thought, she strode right past the table she'd occupied with Nick and flipped her phone out to dial Robyn for a ride home. Wouldn't it be a bummer if she took out these killing urges on her best friend, though? What a waste.

"Hey, wait up." Nick was still tucking his wallet into his back pocket when he caught up to her. "Dessert was supposed to be my treat, by the way."

"I can pay my own way."

"Ah, the prostitution proposition."

When she didn't slow down or even crack a smile, he tugged on her elbow until she stopped.

"Hey. What's going on?"

"I have to go."

"Oh, well, that's fine. I'll take you. Where to?"

"You can't." She turned back to her phone, finger hovering over speed dial.

"Something happened." The stubborn look in his eyes suggested he wasn't dropping the subject until he got a satisfactory answer.

She sighed, frustrated, and flipped the phone shut to face him. "Nick, this—you and me—isn't going to work. I don't...*do* this kind of thing."

He looked confused.

She gave him a straight look. "I'm going to be blunt. I have no desire to compare notes with Shannon and friends."

"So Hillary did follow you in there. I saw her get up right after you did and head in the same direction."

Cassie just looked at him.

"Shannon's friend."

She didn't respond.

He sighed, looking torn. "Okay, it's true that Shannon and I dated, but I refused to have anything to do with her friend. That's the truth. No one believes me when I say it, especially since she keeps swearing that we did. But I swear I didn't sleep with the woman. She's nuts. I feel sorry for her, but hell. Talk about a head case. I've heard about her freaking out other guys, pretending pregnancies, doing stuff like she probably did with you...she's messed up. I stay away from that kind of thing."

"Really?"

"I swear to God. Shannon and I had a casual thing going for a while. I'll admit that. I'm no monk. But that cooled off months ago—and I never had anything to do with Hillary."

Cassie nodded, her anger and jealousy seeping away. Self-preservation, if nothing else, would have kept a footloose guy like Nick away from someone as acquisitive as this Hillary person.

"Does that mean you believe me?"

She shrugged. "Sure."

"Does that mean you'll go out with me?"

Cassie rolled her eyes, suppressing a grin at his unabashedly hopeful smile. "No."

"No?"

She raised an eyebrow. "You really like to push your luck, don't you?"

"It was worth a try. At least let me drive you home. Or wherever you were going."

She pursed her lips wryly and tucked her phone back into her purse. "Home. I had nowhere I needed to be."

"Except away from me."

"I was a little miffed."

He nodded, eyes twinkling. "And now you're not?"

"Now, I'm just exhausted. Socially. First, the speed dating, then the come-on from you and then the curvy duo from hell."

"Curvy duo from hell?"

"I could be exaggerating."

"Could be." He slid a hand under her elbow and casually steered her toward the parking lot. "So, about those Web site lessons."

Cassie glanced at him, remembering. "Right. Tuesday...six-thirty?"

"Great. We could order pizza."

"Yes. You could." For him and Robyn. Cassie had some self-preserving instincts of her own.

# Step 7

*Internet Love—or Intervention, Part Duh*
*Savvy girlfriend also admits to a problem and seeks help*
*from the recovering lovelorn.*

HURRYING UP TO her apartment, Cassie wiped her sweaty palms on her thighs. That had been close. Too close. She'd been so close to agreeing to date Nick. She wanted to, but any idiot could tell that would be a bad move in so many ways.

No, she didn't think he'd been lying about Hillary, but the woman had certainly served as a reminder. St. Louis was full of women who'd no doubt offer their right arm to date a guy like Nick. What guy could resist a selection like that? At the very least, Nick represented a greater risk to Cassie's heart than she was consciously willing to run.

Thank God he'd chimed in about the Web site maintenance lessons, thereby reminding her to set him and Robyn up again. Now all she had to do was make sure Robyn was at her apartment at the appropriate time and Cassie could split and leave them to it. They were both attractive, severely likable people. They'd get together in no time.

At the very least, this setup would reduce Cassie's exposure to temptation. Heaven knew she didn't need to spend more time alone with Nick; given sufficient time and opportunity, Cassie would cave to her longings for sure.

Meanwhile, she needed to do something proactive to keep Nick out of her system. And she was very much afraid she knew what that would be. Up until now, Cassie had only been humoring and accompanying Robyn through her dating adventures. Perhaps it was time to open her own mind and eyes and give the pop-up strategy the chance it deserved.

She was not specifically trolling, never that; trolling for men and commitment would almost certainly interfere with the fate principle and Cassie refused to do that. But it couldn't hurt to invite possibilities. Make herself available.

Perhaps she'd find some guy she could casually date, and thereby take her mind off Nick. Yes. She'd simply take her own advice and find another guy to distract herself from her own two-footed hormonal weakness.

*Not* an addiction. Cassie was *not* addicted to Nick. Just highly susceptible. And that was as far as she was taking it. This time.

"FINE. SIX-THIRTY. I'll be there. Okay." Robyn sounded resigned over the phone. "But Nick's going to be just a bit disappointed when he finds out it's me giving him the lessons in your place."

"He'll get over it. Meanwhile, what other dating possibilities do you have in mind? I'm feeling the need for some male companionship myself."

"You're kidding."

"Nope. I need to start dating again."

"So you're actually serious about this now?" The wry disbelief in Robyn's voice was clear even over the phone line.

"Well, of course. But what do you mean?"

"Cassie, I'm not an idiot. Misguided occasionally, but not an idiot. I know you've been putting up with all my dating adventures out of charity and friendship. You might have suggested that we were both on the lookout for guys, but we weren't. I was looking and you were watching over me. Frankly, I think at least part of that is because you've had your eye on a particular guy, if you'd only admit it."

Cassie groaned. "Oh, I admit it. But that doesn't mean I should do anything about it. Sure, I'm attracted to Nick, but he's the wrong guy at this time for me. We've already talked about this. I'm all over temporary guys. If I go after a guy, it's because I think we have a good shot at a mature relationship, not a fling. Flings are time-consuming and illogical and I don't have the patience for them anymore."

"So why do you keep pushing the idea on me?"

"*You* are trying to get over a serious relationship. *I'm* just trying to distract myself from a physical attraction. Worlds of difference."

"If you say so." Robyn still sounded unconvinced.

"I do. So...what's on the agenda?"

"You won't like it." Now she sounded convinced.

"Try me."

"Cass, just trust me. This isn't for you."

"So what can it hurt to tell me?"

Robyn sighed. "Online dating."

"Eeeew."

"See? You're biased."

"No, I'm not. It's a clashing of worlds for me. I'm just too involved on the Internet—professionally—to turn it into my social arena."

"Okay. But it's helped me a lot. I'm quite the flirt on-line, I'll have you know. I even have an e-boyfriend now." Robyn chuckled.

"Uh-oh."

"Relax. I'm just playing, and 'Man As Island' knows that, too. We're flirting. He's sort of helping me hone my social skills, you know? I'll be a lot more comfortable in person if I can practice this way first."

"'Man as island'?"

"That's his screen name. Man As Island. Get it? We've been chatting back and forth for a few weeks now."

"Interesting." Actually, given the guy's screen name, he sounded like yet another brooding type that Robyn didn't need. "But, what else do you have up your sleeve? We need some face action."

"Well, on Friday night, there's this class someone told me about. Are you interested? I think they have a seat or two open."

"Sure. Whatever. Sign me up." A class. That sounded positive, normal. Yes, she could actually work up some enthusiasm for taking a class and meeting guys and new friends in a semirelaxed atmosphere.

And, sure, she was really just talking herself into

this—but if Robyn was brave enough to put herself out there at Cassie's suggestion, Cassie could do no less. "Okay, okay. Count me in." Desperate and possibly insane, but in.

"YOU'RE NOT ROBYN."

"Should I be?" Nick's eyes, on the other side of her apartment threshold—and more than an hour early for his lesson—twinkled devilishly.

"You're early. Again." All day she'd focused ruthlessly on a set of banners she was constructing for Nick's Web page—while absolutely refusing to picture Nick and Robyn, here, later. Alone. Doing God only knows what....

"Yeah, I've been having trouble getting my computer to work online. It's left me stranded for now, so I thought, What the hell? I'd show up early here and beg for help." He looked hopeful. "Any chance you could swing by the hangar with me and check it out? We can do the lessons from there, couldn't we? I thought it might be even more practical, since that's the machine I'd be using to make changes to the site."

"But, Robyn..."

He raised his brows. "You were expecting company?"

No. Not this early. Rats. "We've been coordinating something for one of my clients and she was just going to drop by today...let me see if I can call her and..."

Moving several feet away for privacy, she dialed Robyn's cell phone and whispered urgently. "Robyn. Come. *Now.*"

"Now?" Robyn spoke in a low voice. "I can't do that. I'm in a meeting."

"A meeting? With whom?"

"Another client. Remember?"

Cassie grumbled. "When's your meeting over?"

Robyn groaned softly. "No time this century. Look, I have to go. I think you're going to have to wing it with Nick. Good luck."

"Robyn—" A click on the line and then a dial tone told Cassie she really was on her own.

"Everything okay?" Nick spoke quietly from behind her.

"I...sure. So. The hangar, huh?"

"Yeah. I can drive."

Well, an airplane hangar—given his feelings about the sanctity of an airplane seat—might be the safest bet for her. Certainly better than being alone with him in her office, a few mere feet from her very own bedroom, thanks. "Sure. Let me just log off the computer...." She did so, feeling his eyes on her all the while, then flashed him a grim smile. "Let's go."

EVEN IN THE DIM EVENING light, Cassie could see the enthusiasm dancing in Nick's eyes as they got close enough to see the airport. This was his world and he loved it, no doubt about it. A plane flew in overhead, low and steady, lights blinking and engine roaring loud enough that Cassie cringed. She expected, at any moment, the pilot to miscalculate and land on the Jeep's nonexistent roof, or maybe right behind them. Talk about the race from hell.

Veering sharply right, to Cassie's silent relief, Nick maneuvered the Jeep along a minor road and into a parking area on the outskirts of the airport. The plane that had flown in overhead landed safely on what was obviously a runway strip and eventually rolled to a stop.

After climbing down from the Jeep, Cassie cautiously followed Nick across the lot's paved expanse. Tracking him by the sound of his footsteps alone, she gazed all around, wide-eyed. The place looked larger than life. Not like a huge international airport—this wasn't Lambert Field, after all—but still, bigger than it looked from the highway. Only a guy like Nick wouldn't be intimidated by it.

Realizing he'd gotten a bit ahead of her, she picked up the pace and followed him into one of the box-like buildings. It was smaller than some of the others, but, naturally, smaller was a relative term. The place was still big enough to house two airplanes and more. One corner had been sectioned off into a makeshift office with a couple of chairs and a desk complete with computer.

"This is it?"

He shrugged. "Have a seat."

"Okay."

She pulled up a chair and he started to do so, then he straightened suddenly on a curse. "I forgot. Let me just give Chad a call, tell him he needs to take my flight in the morning. We're swapping out to accommodate lessons—" He grabbed the phone, spoke quickly with his partner, then hung up. He found Cassie regarding him with a frown.

"What?"

"You fly every day, don't you?"

He shrugged. "Depends on the length of the trip. Sometimes two or even three times a day, if the jobs are minor or the lessons are short."

"In one of those?" She gestured at the planes.

He quirked a half grin. "Well, I wasn't born with wings, so those would be my other options, yes."

She still shook her head, amazed. "I just can't believe you entrust your life to a plane that size. Every day. Sometimes a few times a day."

He shrugged. "It's what I do. I maintain my own planes and I do a damn good job of it. Contrary to popular belief, I can be pretty responsible about such things. Anal even. Just ask Chad. I'm always riding him about maintenance and procedure." Nick grinned. "He calls me the company bureaucrat. And that's on a good day."

"So, you're completely comfortable with it. No fears for your safety. No sense that you've lost control."

"Like I said, I take care of my planes and I'm the pilot. Doesn't get much more in control than that." He smiled at her. "And I think you're speaking from the sidelines, too. Ever been up in a small craft before?"

"Commercial airlines, all the way. So, in a word, *no.*"

"That sounds final." He leaned back in his seat. "Are you afraid?"

"Of flying?" She glanced at the plane. "I've flown before. Several times. And I have a healthy respect for life when I'm up in a plane, but no, I'm not really afraid of flying just to get from one place to the other. I just wonder about the odds. If you're going up, every day, more often than that...don't you think that eventually bad luck's going to catch up with you?"

"There's that fatalism talking again." He smiled. "It's actually a simple matter of mathematics, Cass. Ever study statistics in school?"

She grinned ruefully. "I don't think you can get away from it no matter which major you pick. Yes, I took a stats class or two."

"So you know that a ten percent chance of something happening doesn't mean it will actually happen every tenth opportunity it has. It means, that each opportunity, you've got a ninety percent guarantee that it *won't* happen.

"Hell, think birth control. Condoms have an eighty-something percent success rate, right? But that doesn't mean that ten to twenty percent of couples using them end up pregnant anyway. It means, each time they have sex, a couple can be eighty-some percent sure that nobody's going to get knocked up."

She wrinkled her nose. "No, only fifty percent of us have a chance of getting knocked up."

He rolled his eyes. "Yes, yes, women are saints, men are scum. You get my point, though, right? You face the same odds each time you go up in a plane. They don't get worse just because you go up a lot. If anything, they get better because the pilot has more experience and his plane has all the kinks worked out of it. It's also maintained properly and doesn't sit idle."

She gazed at him shrewdly. "You know, for a guy who dropped out of college, you sure took your studies seriously."

He shrugged. "I may not have gotten the degree, but I've taken some classes since SLU."

"You have?"

He shrugged. "Some correspondence classes, some night school. I needed the business know-how."

"So you have most of an engineering degree, several business classes mastered and you fly planes. Do you also knit?"

He laughed, his cheeks actually a little ruddy. "Got a nice scarf coming along back at home if you'd like to check it out."

She rolled her eyes at his lame comeback and spoke quietly. "You surprise me."

"Good. Maybe I can surprise you about other things."

She gave him a suspicious look.

He grinned devilishly. "I'm just inviting you to fly with me. Want to?"

"You want me to fly with you. In that dinky little plane of yours." She gave him a disbelieving look. "Seriously."

"Seriously."

"Just because. Just like that."

He shrugged. "I have a minor freight trip to make. I was going to do it in the morning, but it wouldn't take much to do it this evening instead. Actually, I'd postponed it to make time for your Web site lessons." He gave her a boyish smile. "I could just switch it back. Re-submit the original flight plan."

"And I'd come with you."

"Yep. Having a hard time with this, are we?" He gave her a patronizing look that made her eyes narrow.

"Just getting my facts straight before I decide how much of an idiot I want to be."

He smiled, still a little condescending. "And the verdict…"

The condescending did it. "Fine. You're on. Take me up, Flyboy. But no loops. I'm not one of your geriatric hornballs and I *don't* have a death wish."

"Great." He bounced out of his seat and yanked up the phone to make a few calls. Less than an hour later, they were climbing into his plane and Cassie was entrusting her life to a cowboy in the sky.

"I'm going to regret this, aren't I." Her heart was pounding, but if she were honest, she'd have to admit that it was at least sixty percent excitement. Maybe more. The odds were good she'd enjoy herself. She grinned wryly to herself.

"Relax, Cassie. I know what I'm doing."

"Um, Nick. You checked the plane out, right?"

He gave her a curious look. "Thoroughly. You stood there and watched me, remember?"

"Uh-huh. Nick, that door rattled when you closed it. You know that? You're taking us up into the sky with a rattling door. If that thing opened, we'd both get sucked out of the plane and plunge to horrible deaths. Right?"

He grinned. "I suppose it could happen. If the plane

flew high enough. Whoosh and one hell of a ride down."

"I'm serious. I've seen sturdier doors attached to a fence post."

He sighed. "Relax, Cassie. First of all, a plane this size doesn't fly high enough that the cockpit would need to be pressurized, so there would be no 'whoosh' effect if the door—against all odds—flew open or busted off. It'd get a little bit windy in here, but we just *might* escape death by whoosh. And second, yes, the door is light. It's light so we can fly. Logical? But it won't open midflight and we're not going to die."

"You're sure?"

He raised his brows. "You want statistics again?"

"Are they in terms of hundreds?"

He grinned. "Probably not."

She made a face. "At least you're honest. Fine. What do I do first?"

"Get in. We always fly inside of the plane. Safer that way."

She gave him a look.

"Step here." He pointed to the wheel and she put her foot on top of the step and climbed in. She sat down and fumbled nervously for her seat belt. After she'd fastened it, Nick reached in and took his sweet time checking for fit and security.

Nervous, she almost missed the glitter of deviltry in his eyes as he smoothed the strap over one hip. "Nice. Really nice."

She narrowed her eyes at him.

"Nice fit. The seat belt, I mean." He gave her an innocent look that fooled her no more than hers had once fooled him.

"Fly, Cowboy."

She heard him laughing as he shut the door and jogged around the nose of the plane to climb in on the other side.

Cassie, trying to pretend this was just an ordinary flight, or even just a car trip, jumped when Nick leaned out his window and yelled "Clear." Then the engine roared on. The thing was loud. Really loud. She watched, nervously, as Nick ran through a series of checks, pushing pedals and fiddling with the yoke. A similar set of pedals and yoke arranged in front of her moved in tandem with his set. Damn, if she was the "co-pilot" of this operation, they were in serious trouble.

"Ready?" He raised his voice above the roar of the plane.

She nodded but it was a lie. As Nick adjusted his headset and spoke into a microphone, the plane started moving. Oh, God. It was small. Really small. Small and *loud*. The stupid thing really was a car. And now it was going to try to fly? She gritted her teeth. The thing bounced all over the place. Cassie thought perhaps it might really be a large clumsy tricycle or, at most, a Jeep that wanted to be a plane when it grew up.

Jeep or plane, it turned onto the runway, paused, then roared to a higher pitch before bumping and rattling and bouncing its way down the too short strip that, on second thought, just *couldn't* be a runway. Cassie gripped the seat. She was going to die.

As the plane's speed increased even more, she grew a little less afraid. The madly bouncing contraption would pitch violently onto its side and/or combust before it ever left the ground. At least death on sweet soil would be immediate. Falling from the sky, terrified and fully cognizant of her impending doom...not good.

After a last, bone-rattling lurch, the ride smoothed suddenly, they tipped alarmingly backward and Cassie saw more of the sky than she'd expected. They were airborne. Oh, shit.

The ride was still bumpy, but as they ascended and leveled out, the turbulence lessened and Cassie chanced another breath. And then another.

Nick shot her a quick glance. "You okay?"

She nodded, still unable to speak without squeaking, but she began to believe she might live through this. If she didn't consider the landing in advance.

Actually, riding in the plane now, after that horrible trek down the runway...was sort of like dragging a flimsy old canoe across a rocky embankment, quite sure something so clumsy couldn't be seaworthy, then suddenly realizing it was just fine in the water. It was built for water. Likewise, the plane was built for flying—not rolling along a runway for any length of time.

It could be okay.

Feeling braver, Cassie chanced a look out the window and, wincing with excitement and a thrill of fear, she looked down. It was amazing. So much more real than on a big commercial jet. She really had a sense of flying through the sky, with air and clouds around them and the earth far below. Wow. No wonder he loved it, daredevil that he was. It was larger than life.

She glanced over at him, mirroring the smile she saw on his face. He was happy up here.

She cleared her throat. At a shout, her voice might not reveal her fears. "How long is the flight?"

"About an hour. But it's a quick turnaround. We're just dropping off a couple boxes, readying the plane for return flight and heading back home again. Okay?"

She nodded. That would put them back in St. Louis at around nine o'clock, leaving their Web site lessons too late, but it was worth it. Well worth it. "This is amazing, Nick."

"Huh?" He cupped a hand over his ear.

She raised her voice. "Flying. I like it."

He smiled widely. "I thought you might."

It was beautiful, too. They were flying into the sunset and the colors and the wisping of clouds looked surreal, from a little girl's fantasyland of pastel rainbows and soft fluffs of magic. Cassie expected a Pegasus unicorn to overtake them at any moment. She smiled at her own whimsy.

They didn't speak much during the flight as Nick seemed to understand what she was experiencing. She wondered if it was this magical for him every time. If it was the same, different or better. It was freeing, thrilling, scary and beautiful.

After a while she realized exactly what was at the root of the experience. Aside from the tangible beauty of the sky and the real sense of being so far above the ground, she realized that part of the thrill was that she'd trusted Nick. Given up complete control of their lives to him—and then relaxed into it. There was a thrilling freedom in doing just that. Reveling in the risk and the trust...it was addictive.

She winced at her choice of phrase and refused to let it interfere with her enjoyment. Nick had given her a precious gift, little did he know it. She smiled, wasn't surprised when he paused briefly to return it. Or maybe he did know it.

A while later Cassie was more than ready to recant every positive sentiment about this whole experience. It was time to land and land they must. On a commercial jet, she never saw the nose of the plane seeking nothing more than to crash into solid land. In Nick's Cessna, Cassie expected life as she knew it to end in a deafening explosion, metal flying everywhere, balls of fire, body parts, pain...

Still, they descended and, despite her fears, after one terrifying lurch, she felt the blessed familiarity of the plane's wheels bumping wildly down the runway. Cassie realized she might live to see another day.

The flight home was yet a different experience, but less realistic since they were in the dark and, once they took off, Cassie could pretend they were really on an airline jet making a routine flight. The lights below looked much as they did on a larger craft and Cassie was free to experience the sights and sounds inside the plane. On that thought, she tried desperately to concentrate on the hardware and mechanics of the craft, but found her gaze constantly straying to the pilot instead.

Nick looked capable, cocky and heartbreakingly hot

in the pilot's seat. Competence was so sexy in a man. Intelligence, sense of humor...he was more temptation than she thought she'd have to resist. Especially in the glow of tiny lights inside the cockpit and the stars and moon beyond.

It was a lot for a girl to take in in one evening.

The landing, at least—dear God, not again—helped disrupt the fantasy. She stared as the ground seemed to rise up to meet them. Finally, after an eternity of sweaty, heart-pounding terror, Cassie watched, transfixed, as the plane touched, lurched, then wildly rumbled its way down the runway. She went limp with relief. When the plane stopped and she finally climbed out of her seat and down from the plane, her knees gave momentarily.

Nick, chuckling a little, wrapped an arm around her waist to steady her.

"Sorry." She uttered the word on a thread of sound.

"Don't worry about it. You did great." He squeezed her waist in a one-armed hug that she couldn't protest. Nor did she want to. She was still adjusting to the continuation of life.

"So you liked it? Except for the landing?"

"Oh, sure. And I really liked the landing. The fact that we were able to do it. Twice."

He laughed. "I admit I was shaky the first time I landed in something this small. It's easier if you understand the mechanics and physics behind it, though. That the rattles and bumps are because of the plane's size and proximity to the ground. That they're normal and the plane is built for it. If you know why certain things are and what's been done to compensate for their effects, even use them to the plane's advantage...it's easier."

He cleared his throat. "And, um, that was actually a damn smooth landing, I'll have you know. Especially considering that I had you in the plane with me. Performance anxiety."

She rolled her eyes, realizing he was trying to steady her still. Very sweet of him. "I'm sure it was, Cowboy. Thanks for not killing me." She paused, let sincerity creep into her voice. "And thanks for the ride. It was amazing."

He smiled. "I'm glad you enjoyed it."

"So. About your Web site lesson."

He glanced at her, startled. "You're still up for it?"

She shrugged. "Well, I can at least get you online decently and give you the basics tonight."

"With...pizza, maybe?"

She laughed. "Please. I'm starving."

"You got it."

While Nick arranged for the pizza, Cassie settled herself at his computer. She turned it on, tried to go online and kept getting an error message. Frowning, she got up, checked the connection to the computer, then followed a long phone line—the thing had obviously been rigged pretty crudely—to the wall.

She shot Nick a suspicious look. "Your modem was unplugged."

Nick, who'd just set the phone back in its ancient cradle, glanced up. His cheeks grew just a little ruddy. "Um...unplugged?"

"Unplugged." She wiped her hands together to rid them of dust and strode toward him. "I don't suppose you'd know anything about that."

"Er...no?"

She raised an eyebrow.

He gave her a sheepish look. "Well, maybe I got the error message and didn't bother to question it. I didn't check. I could have, but if I had..."

"Mmm. The modern-day equivalent to accidentally running out of gas?"

He shoved his hands into his pockets. "Could I have gotten you to myself today if I hadn't?"

"No. Probably not." She softened her stance. "And I admit I'm glad that you did."

He blinked, obviously surprised by the reprieve. "Yeah?"

"Yeah. That plane ride, Nick. It really was amazing."

A slow smile spread across his face until his eyes were dancing delightedly. "You really liked it that much?"

She gave him a rueful look. "Enough that I won't question the modem any further."

"Cool."

"Don't push it. Come on, Cowboy. Let's talk Web site maintenance."

Forty-five minutes later Cassie had to admit that Nick had more patience and a quicker mind than she'd credited. They'd gone through a lot more than she'd intended to cover in twice the amount of time. Or, rather, what *Robyn* would have covered in that amount of time.

They paused only briefly for pizza before resuming

lessons and Cassie was almost disappointed to realize that Nick really was sincere about wanting to learn to maintain his site. Not just a stud on the make.

"Wow. Eleven o'clock." Cassie blinked at her watch. "I'm sorry, Nick, but—"

"No, I'm sorry. I didn't know it was so late. I was just starting to get the hang of it and I guess I got all excited about it and forgot the time." He gave her a boyish grin. "Come on. I'll take you home." Cassie followed him out to his car.

When they arrived at her apartment, despite her protests, he walked her upstairs. She unlocked her door, flipped on the light switch, then turned to face Nick.

It was jarring. She'd grown so used to sitting next to him, working with him, that she'd almost forgotten the kind of wallop he could pack face-to-face. There was certainly more depth to the man than she'd previously suspected, but there was no denying the stud factor, either.

"Cass." He spoke softly. "I know none of this was in your plans, but I want you to know I really had a good time tonight."

"So did I." She'd be lying if she suggested otherwise. "That plane ride...well, let's just say I could see where you'd love flying enough to pursue it like you did."

He shrugged. "A man's nothing without his passions. I guess I just saw no good reason not to pursue what I wanted. Like now."

Cassie gulped. The man's timing was exquisite. Hadn't even seen that one coming.

"I'd like to see you again."

She cleared her throat. "Well, there's still the Web site lessons. Probably need one more to cover everything we didn't get to. I still owe you…"

"And I'll take it if that's all I can get. But I'm talking about a personal relationship, Cass. Nothing blurry about it. You and me. On a date. Even something as ordinary as dinner and a movie. Or the zoo. Anything. What about this weekend?"

"Nick—"

"Cassie." Quick as anything, he'd slid forward, cupped her cheeks and took her lips with his. She froze, then melted. As quickly as he'd moved, she might have expected something rougher, but this…this was seduction, sneaky and yet cranked for maximum effect.

His lips were soft against hers, caressing slowly, before he slanted his mouth against her slackened lips and slipped his tongue between them. Gentle, exploring, seducing, knowing. The man had skill. It was drugging, mesmerizing. She could go under, fast.

She got out—quick. Still breathing heavily, she held him off with both hands against his chest.

His eyes dark and probing, he held her gaze. "Cassie. Go out with me."

She studied his handsome face, flushed cheeks, nostrils flared with his quickened breathing, his eyes. Beyond the arousal, they were sincere and allowed no bullshit. So she wouldn't give him any. "No. I'm sorry, but no."

"Why? Don't tell me you're not interested."

She grinned wryly, her heart still shuddering in her chest. "I wouldn't dare to presume, Cowboy."

He smiled slightly. "So?"

"Nick. I can't go out with you. You have the potential to break my heart and screw up my life. I don't intend to let you do that." She raised an eyebrow. "Is that honest enough for you?"

His eyes widened and he stepped forward again.

She held him off. "Good night, Nick."

"But—"

Gently she closed the door against him and latched it. Ugh. Honesty could be so painful. But sometimes that kind of honesty—the commitment-threatening kind— was what it took. Surely, Nick would run for cover now.

# Step 8

*Sports for Idiots*
*We educate ourselves before returning to*
*the field of our defeat.*

"SO, HOW DID THE WEB SITE lessons go Tuesday night?" Robyn gave Cassie a teasing, speculative look as she dropped her purse on the couch.

Cassie was almost ready, concentrating on a coat of mascara before blinking owlishly into the mirror. She looked good. She thought so, anyway, despite the tossing and turning these past few nights. Sexual frustration would eventually take its toll on her looks.

Sexual frustration, however, wasn't something *she* should have had to deal with this week—at least not to this extent. Tuesday night, as much as she might now dislike the idea, was supposed to have been a first date for Nick and Robyn.

She tossed Robyn a knowing glance. "I think a better question would be, Was there really a client that day? *You* were supposed to be giving the Web site lessons, not me."

"Sure, the meeting was legit. Although, I admit I might have made it up if it weren't." Robyn gave her an unabashed grin.

Cassie sighed. "The lessons were good. The flight was amazing."

"Flight? You flew? *With Nick?*"

Cassie smiled, unable to mask her enjoyment of the experience. "Yeah. Nick took me on one of his freight delivery trips. It was incredible. I can see how he would be so passionate about it."

Robyn cocked her head a moment, considering her friend with an intrigued look on her face. "Amazing. So tell me about the passionate part."

"*Robyn.* We just flew. And then I gave him the lessons he was promised. And we had pizza because it was late and neither one of us had had dinner."

"Sounds like an awesome date."

Cassie gave her a startled look. "It wasn't a date. It just happened."

"Sure it did."

"It *did*. A date is something you set up in advance with the intention of furthering a relationship. Getting to know someone."

"So you didn't get to know Nick better?"

That gave Cassie pause. Actually she had gotten to know him better. She really had. Being up in the plane with him, she felt as though she'd had a deep, monumentally important glimpse inside his heart and soul. She'd probably learned more about him in one night than she would learn on a dozen ordinary dates with another man.

And then the kiss at the door...oh, my. Talk about fantasy material. *Don't go there, Cass.* She suppressed further imaginings and focused on the here and now.

Sure, Nick was excellent fantasy material. Furthering a relationship, however, had not been the original intent of the evening. "It still wasn't a date."

"Whatever you say." The lilt in Robyn's voice, not to mention the smug curve of her mouth, suggested she'd believe what she wanted.

Cassie just gave her an exasperated look but failed to totally meet Robyn's eyes. Time to change the subject. "So tell me about this class we're going to attend. Where are they having it?"

Robyn shrugged, but her eyes were still knowing. "The class is one of those just-for-fun events. It's called Sports 101 and..."

Cassie did a double take. "Sports?" Then she started laughing. "Are you serious?"

Robyn raised her nose self-righteously. "Fine, laugh if you must, but after the sports bar incident, I decided it would be appropriate. Double duty. Meet guys and do penance at the same time."

"And will we meet guys at this class? Where is it?"

"Probably not, but they have happy hour right after, and guys show up for that. Um, Cass...the class is at the same sports bar...."

Cassie groaned, remembering the butt-ugly-blue incident. "I might have known. Heck, we were probably the inspiration for this class. So, will they hurt us?"

"Aw, live dangerously, Cass."

"Hey, you were blessedly drunk for most of the experience. *I* was the one in excruciating social discomfort."

"I know, I know. It was ugly." Sighing, obnoxiously

bored with the subject, Robyn tossed Cassie's purse at her and picked up her own.

"A little lingering *gratitude* wouldn't be out of line." Pouting still, Cassie slung the purse over her shoulder and followed Robyn out the door. "If you get drunk tonight I'm throwing you to the wolves."

"So, LADIES. Let's hear it again...." Shoving his paunch aside, the still-attractive former baseball player settled a foot atop a chair seat. Strangely enough, the pose did look manly. Cassie frowned, pondering.

"...batter of the opposing team's up. The opposing team's two runs ahead. Pitcher throws and the batter drops to the ground. You say..."

"*He took a dive!*"

"*Faker!*"

"*Let 'im have it in the teeth next time!*"

The man rubbed his hands together. "Excellent, excellent. Moving along. Quiz—we have three runners on base and the batter hits the ball into the stands directly behind center field. What do we have?"

"*Home run!*"

"*Happy fans—get the ball, quick!*"

"And?" The man raised his eyebrow.

"A headache." Cassie muttered it, but saw his gaze light on her with mild disapproval.

"It's called a grand-slam home run. Four runs come in, four points. Fans are more than happy—they're screaming and dancing and chanting in the stands."

"*Ooooh.*"

Cassie swore she saw several women jotting furiously with pens and pencils.

"Some basics...how many innings are there in professional baseball and what constitutes an inning?"

Cassie's brain numbed. Did none of these women ever suffer through a game? Had none of them even paid attention in high-school Phys. Ed.? She wasn't particularly fond of sports, but she hadn't grown up under a rock, either.

"You. The blonde in the back. Like the skirt. What's an inning?"

Cassie blinked owlishly.

"He means you, dummy." Robyn elbowed her, laughing under her breath.

"This is your fault," she muttered back. "Why do you always get me in trouble?" Louder, she responded, "Nine innings. Each team gets a turn at bat in each inning."

"Excellent." His gaze rested on her for a moment before he moved reluctantly on to the next topic. "A foul ball is..."

Cassie crossed her legs more securely, her cheeks flushed, and shot Robyn a look. "He can see up my skirt, can't he."

Robyn laughed some more. "Hush."

"Is this almost over?"

Unexpectedly, the instructor responded to her question. "Yes. It's over in five minutes. But only if you can tell me the names of three of our local professional sports teams."

Cassie rolled her eyes. "Ask Robyn here."

Obediently, Robyn stood up. "Baseball, the Cardinals. Football, the Rams. Hockey, the Blues." She sat down, primly, smugly. She was congratulated and "class" was dismissed to happy hour.

Cassie glanced over, surprised and deflated. "You did do penance."

Robyn tucked her tongue in cheek. "Hey, in my shoes, wouldn't you do a little homework before showing up here for this?"

Cassie grumbled.

"Besides, I had help." Robyn stuck a thumb past her shoulder, pointing at the door, and Cassie followed it, already suspecting. "I read lips. Especially lips as fine as that set."

Nick smiled innocently at Cassie from across the crowd of women and she closed her eyes on a rueful grin. She couldn't escape the man. Should she continue to try? Was it a useless endeavor? Maybe he wasn't a distraction.

Maybe she kept running into him for a reason and trying to avoid Nick amounted to bucking her own fate, which maybe she shouldn't do—

"Hey, ladies."

Cassie opened her eyes to see a vaguely familiar face. Not Nick. This guy was about their age and blond, with good-ol'-boy looks, beefy verging on fat from a few too many beers, but cheerful and good-looking nonetheless.

"Remember me?"

Cassie squinted, rearranging the picture slightly, elongating and debleaching the buzz-cut hair, to...

"Cha-ad?" Another voice piped up behind him. "And Jerry." She smiled for real. "Well, hi, guys. How's it going? Wow, I haven't seen you since..."

Jerry elbowed his way forward to give her a shaming look. "Since you stopped coming to the lovely Becky's parties."

Cassie gave him a droll look, which dragged a bigger grin out of his freckled face before he continued. "We've been waiting up at the bar and I took a minute to phone somebody else I thought you'd remember...."

Ah. That would be the *reason*. Nothing magical about a tip from a buddy. "Was it Nick, by any chance?" She glanced over her shoulder, saw Nick steadily weaving his way toward them. Several women seemed to be stalling out his approach, no doubt eager to show off their newfound knowledge.

"Yep." Jerry's eyes brightened as he looked past Cassie. "Is this our Robyn? The beauteous art student? We love art students."

Robyn rolled her eyes, but played along with Jerry's obvious foolishness. "Hi, Jerry, you idiot."

"I love you, too." He gave her a mock adoring look, making her laugh. His eyes widened comically as he focused on the beer in Robyn's hand. "Look out. Robyn, darling, step *away* from the alcohol. There will be no table dancing from you tonight, young lady."

Robyn rolled her eyes, but she was grinning. "Nothing like a couple of clowns to remind you of your weaknesses."

He gave her a pitying look. "And, oh, but you have a big one."

"Shut up and find me a chair." But she was laughing.

"The lady has spoken." He bobbed his head in mock obedience and gestured her before him. "Let's go snag a table." Jerry glanced back over his shoulder. "Yo, Chad, pick up the pace. We need you for height. The place is filling up. Look high, look low…" Jerry snagged Chad's arm and Cassie made to follow—

"Cassie," a low voice murmured in her ear from behind.

She caught her breath on a half squeak. "Don't *do* that."

"Scare you?" He grinned at her, still close, and cupped her bare shoulders.

And then some. It was as though his voice, coupled with his warm breath along her neck and earlobe, flipped a switch and now her hormones were partying like it was 1999 all over again. Then add his hands on her skin—

"Yes, you scared me." She moved slightly away, playing for space and sanity.

"Weren't you going to wait for me?"

She cast a gaze up and down his fine body, trying desperately not to pause anywhere in between. "You look like a big boy to me. I thought you could find your own way."

"Still scared?"

She faltered a little. *Yes.*

He moved slightly closer again. "Ah, come on, Cass. It's a crowded bar, getting more crowded by the second. Looks pretty safe to me."

She glanced around. It was crowded now. Nothing

intimate about a bar. Maybe, if she wasn't quite sure, if she thought that...this might be the best way to test the waters. Again.

"Have a drink with me." He glanced around, laid his hand possessively on a small, still unoccupied table.

"But Chad and Jerry and Robyn..."

"Know exactly where we are and why." He gave her a no-nonsense look that discouraged any foolish arguments.

Okay, she was a big girl, too. All grown up and well able to handle herself with a man, even one as good-looking as Nick. Especially in a crowded bar. "Okay. A drink."

"Good." They settled into chairs and a fast-moving waitress took their orders and quickly returned with drinks.

After she left, Cassie turned back to Nick, who regarded her with a smug grin. She gave him a narrow-eyed look. "What?"

"This is a date."

"Is not."

"Is, too. And you didn't scare me away the other night." He gestured toward her with his long-neck beer bottle before taking a swig. "I know that's what you were trying to do."

It was. But she'd also been telling the truth. She studied him a moment. "But why?"

"Why what?"

"Why aren't you scared and why on earth do you still want to date me? I'm not Shannon or anything like her. I don't do one-night thrills as a matter of course and no way would somebody mistake me for centerfold material."

He raised his brows. "If I wanted to date Shannon, I would." Then he grinned and ran a caressing gaze over what he could see of her figure. "And as far as that centerfold comment, well, I beg to differ."

She tried to ignore the warmth pooling in her belly. "So what are you doing, then?"

He smiled. "Pursuing my passion."

"Pursuing your..."

"Passion. You. Can you think of any reason why I shouldn't?"

She inhaled sharply, was about to speak when she heard a barrage of voices nearing them. A crowd brushed by, with Robyn among them.

Cassie glanced up, still startled. "Where are you going?"

Robyn stopped and grinned. "Chad's. We ran into some other people he knows—mostly guys—and we're taking the party over there. More room. Come on."

Cassie glanced at Nick, who'd never gotten his answer. He'd obviously abandoned the question for the moment. No doubt he considered it rhetorical.

She didn't. Not quite. Not yet.

"Party at Chad's." Nick smiled at her, memories lingering in his eyes. No doubt he remembered another party, at an apartment he and Jerry had shared with Chad and another fraternity brother seven years ago. He would also remember how it had almost ended.

How it could end now.

"Sounds like a plan." His voice lowered. "You can ride with me."

"Um, no." Momentary panic set in. "I have to stop by my apartment. For something. It's simpler if I just drive. Robyn rode with me anyway." She glanced up. Robyn just shrugged and nodded. Cassie turned her gaze back to Nick.

"But you'll come to the party?" His dark eyes were compelling.

She took a deep breath, eyes still on Nick's, and exhaled slowly, feeling a little reckless. A lot foolish.

"Yes."

# _____Step 9_____

*Parties, Parodies and Perverts*
*We consider alternate avenues of self-destruction.*

"ANYTHING WRONG, ROBYN? You haven't said a word since we left my apartment."

Cassie looked over the car at her friend as she slammed her door shut. Robyn had come upstairs with her and had stopped to check her e-mail while Cassie freshened up and searched frantically for her courage. Robyn had been quiet ever since then.

"Not a thing. Let's go."

Cassie shrugged and joined Robyn. A guy she'd never met opened the door and they walked in. The party was quite a bit larger than the group who had left the bar together. She did see Chad and Jerry, but they were in opposite corners of the living room, each surrounded by an impassable wall of bodies, some of them dancing.

"So. This is Chad's place." Cassie glanced around cautiously. From what she could see, the place had a bifurcation problem. Split personalities.

"He and Jerry live together."

That explained the problem. Part of the decor was techno-wizardry with lots of chrome and contemporary furniture all worshiping the resident, state-of-the-art electronics. The other half wished desperately to be an old-fashioned, hardwood-paneled bar. Heavy wooden stools and fully stocked bar, stained-glass accents. She saw one of those hula girl bobble-heads moving gently to the beat broadcast by its stereo-speaker stage.

"They make the modern-day odd couple." Cassie surprised a grin out of even distracted Robyn. Something was up with her. Cassie just knew it. Why wouldn't she talk about it this time?

"Mmm. Seems to work for them." Robyn glanced around the room, gaze darting to and fro, never quite landing but always seeking.

"Okay, Robyn, spill it. What's going on? Are you up to something?"

She glanced back at Cassie, a little startled. "Scoping? Same as has been going on for a while now? I don't know. What exactly do you mean?"

Maybe that's all it was. Maybe Robyn's confidence was building and she was focusing more. Except focus and frenzied tunnel vision were not exactly the same thing and Robyn's concentration amounted to the latter.

"You'd tell me if something were wrong, wouldn't you?"

"Probably." Robyn raised her chin, obviously scanning the crowd before settling her gaze on a group of guys nearby.

"Probably? What does that mean?"

Robyn grinned ruefully without diverting her attention from the males. "It means I'd avoid a lecture if necessary and avoid hurting or disappointing you if I could." When Cassie, freshly alarmed, would have interrupted, Robyn just held up a hand. "Don't ask and I won't tell. Come on. Let's go meet those guys."

"But—"

"Lighten up, Cass. I've been doing some research and I want to try some stuff out."

"Research? But—"

"Yeah, you'd be absolutely shocked if you knew the twisted things that turn some guys on." She dragged Cassie with her across the room and, just before they were within earshot, she murmured to Cassie, "Whatever I do, just play along. Trust me." In a louder voice with a high-beam smile, she greeted the guys. "Hey, how's it going?"

"Great, great. Glad you came over to join us." A stocky brunette standing closest to them elbowed a distracted friend and all three turned smiles on Cassie and Robyn.

As Cassie smiled back, she caught sight of Nick a few groups away from her. He looked as though he'd been watching her since she walked in. She should go to him. She should. Probably. Why was she chicken all of a sudden? Wasn't she an adult?

"Cass."

"Hmm?" She glanced distractedly at Robyn and realized she'd probably tried repeatedly to get Cassie's attention. "Sorry. I was spacing."

"I was just introducing you around to the guys." She smiled at the three. "This is my friend Cassie."

"Hi, Cassie." The brunette smiled at her while the blonde seemed to focus on Robyn. Cassie proceeded with the usual pleasantries, discussing job and lifestyles with the guys, who all seemed relatively normal. Through it all, she kept half an ear on Robyn's conversation and half an eye on Nick. She was beginning to feel somewhat scattered because of it all.

Robyn seemed quite pleased with herself, however. Actually, now that Cassie thought about it, this was the guy who had walked Robyn out of the bar...

"So, are you free for tomorrow evening?" the blonde, whose eyes still scanned the room, murmured to Robyn.

"Um, sure, I think so." Robyn replied with the same, casual air. Nothing better to do, but might as well go out, they seemed to be saying to each other. Robyn touched Cassie's arm before continuing. "Just give me a moment alone with Cass first? We like to okay these things between us. Just to keep hurt feelings and jealousy to a minimum." She gave him a coyly apologetic look, then tugged a bewildered Cassie a step or two to the side.

Cassie, concerned they were still within earshot, murmured low. "Um, what's up? He seemed nice enough. Couldn't hurt to go out with him. Do you need a pep talk, is that it?"

Robyn moved closer and patted Cassie's shoulder before speaking in an easily audible tone. "No, sweetheart, this is nothing against you, I swear. He just seems really nice. And I've always said this thing between you and me was...just a diversion. A novelty. Kind of a fling? You were okay with that before."

"Uh...*huh?*" Cassie felt gooseflesh popping up all

over her arms. *Sweetheart?* Robyn had totally lost it. Maybe she was seeing things? People?

Robyn raised her eyebrows, didn't drop the smile, then discreetly mouthed the words "play along."

"You've got to be kidding." Cassie didn't bother to lower her voice. "But they're going to think..."

"That what we have together is cheap? Oh, but that's wrong, honey. You know that." Her words still audible to their audience, Robyn gave her such a tender look that Cassie reared back in alarm.

"Kiss me and die." Cassie growled it under her breath.

Robyn choked slightly, her eyes dancing. Cassie could only imagine the look on her own face. Then a movement off to her left caught Cassie's eye and she glanced up distractedly, then back to Robyn, then back, with horror, to see Nick staring at them. He was within earshot—Cassie wasn't sure when that had happened—but even more telling, his eyes had that glazed-over look, cheeks slightly flushed...the *pervert*.

Cassie spoke in a hoarse whisper to Robyn. "Oh, my God. This actually works. Who knew?" She discreetly cast another glance, this time at the three guys Robyn had been targeting. Formerly cool and casual to the point of being jaded, the three now couldn't seem to take their hungry gazes off Robyn's hand. On Cassie's shoulder. Cassie stepped slightly away from Robyn, looking at her friend in mingled amusement and shock. She spoke in a soft murmur punctuated with horrified squeaks. "They're like puppies now. They love the idea of you and me..."

Robyn nodded, obviously triumphant and suppressing outrageous laughter. She mouthed again "play along."

Cassie's eyes widened and she spoke in a firm, no-nonsense tone that was not in the least bit muffled. "Oh, no, baby. I love you and I'd do just about anything for you, but not this. No how, no way."

Cassie heard her own words in recall and panicked. "No. I didn't mean it like that. I mean, I love you, like *platonically*. Remember? Hello?" But her protests, hoarse and squeaking with shock, couldn't register above a whisper. The three guys were still fixated, still half slobbering on themselves as they hung on every gesture, every audible, misguiding word. Then, squeamish, Cassie turned to focus on Nick.

Who looked flushed, his eyes bright and dancing...and his shoulders shaking with outrageous laughter of his own. When he began his approach, Cassie froze, then shifted slightly away from Robyn. Tried to brace herself for whatever outrageousness was headed her way. But it wasn't going to work. Wasn't even going to *begin* to work. *Shit.*

"Well, hi, ladies. Decided to come out of the closet, have we?" Speaking in a loud, hearty voice, he clapped a gentle hand on Cassie's shoulder and one on Robyn's. "Now there's no need to fight over these gentlemen over here. I'm sure they won't mind if you continue to see each other on the side."

Cassie glared. Nick had figured out Robyn's scam and was currently entertaining himself—and several onlookers—to the hilt.

He smiled in wicked anticipation. "So, why don't we all kiss and make up?"

Cassie growled low, ready to let fly with some choice suggestions of her own, when Robyn verbally leaped in.

"I— I have to go. Now. Really."

Cassie glanced up, saw Robyn looking as panicked as she had felt a moment ago. Apparently even Robyn had discovered her limits. Though mollified, Cassie still couldn't help provoking her just a bit. "You sure about that?" She raised an eyebrow. *"Sweetheart?"*

"Um. Yeah. I'm sure." Robyn cleared her throat, glanced briefly and apologetically at Cassie, then slanted an even quicker glance at Nick's earlobe before looking away again. "Actually, I...have a date."

When Robyn looked up again, eyes wide and vulnerable, Cassie dropped the pose and the humor. "A date. You mean slobberface back there?" Cassie pointed to the blond onlooker for whom Robyn had staged this whole fiasco.

Robyn stared blankly. "Who? *Him?* No. Oh, no. I mean..." She sighed, grinned ruefully. "No, not him. I should never have...I guess I'll have to just slip out when he's not looking...I don't know...never mind." She waved a hand, her gaze steering clear of the blonde. "No, I actually have a date with my online guy. If you can believe it." Robyn gave a nervous laugh, completely unlike her usual self.

"With your online guy? But you never said anything..." Cassie narrowed her eyes. "Wait a minute. Is that why you've been acting so weird since we left my apartment?"

"Well...yes. I checked my e-mail, and..." Robyn took a deep breath, held it briefly, then let it out. "I'm supposed to meet Man As Island at a bar near here. About half an hour from now. I was going to go and then I wasn't going to go. I've been waffling about it all day. Then the e-mail again from him." Robyn shook her head, obviously just this side of waffling. "I just didn't want to ruin the fantasy, I guess, but now...well, no offense, Cassie, but..."

Cassie snorted.

Robyn gave her a weak grin. "I guess maybe you and the three puppies over there...and Nick..." She flashed an apologetic glance upward, still unable to meet Nick's eyes, before turning back to Cassie. "I guess the...shock... or strangeness...has popped something into place in this foolish head of mine. I don't want that guy...whatsisface... slobberface."

Robyn took a deep breath before continuing. "In fact, I don't want any guy here or any guy I've seen since we started this whole dating thing. God knows what's come over me these past weeks. And now this act, oh, my God..." She shook her head helplessly, grinning ruefully and obviously a little appalled at her own behavior. "But I know what I want now and what I need to do. I'm going to go meet my online guy. Finally. It's time to take things offline and see if he's real. See if he's really the kind of guy I think he is."

Cassie frowned, concerned, and sensed Nick moving closer to her. He placed a comforting hand on Cassie's shoulder. With effort, she maintained her focus. "You're sure? You hardly know this guy. Do you really want to meet him alone the first time? We can ditch this place and I can follow you to this bar and hang discreetly in the background or something, if that would work. Just in case you need me."

"Are you kidding? With all our late-night chats and long e-mails, I feel like I know this guy better than I knew...Alex. The supposed love of my life." Robyn looked a little floored by the idea, then shrugged and smiled. "So, I'll stop hiding behind you and my screen name and all this craziness—" She gestured around the room, grinning a bit at her disappointed puppies.

Robyn cleared her throat self-consciously. "Um, I guess I did manage to live up to the 'annoying' part of your pop-up analogy, after all...didn't I?"

Cassie snorted and rolled her eyes. "You have no idea." But she was still concerned. "You're really sure about all this?"

Robyn nodded decisively. "It's time I meet him face-to-face."

"Oh, but what if—"

Nick touched her arm. "Let her go, Cass." He was looking at Robyn, an eyebrow raised. "Looks like this is something she needs to do."

Robyn smiled at him, finally meeting his eyes, and accepted the hand he offered. "No hard feelings?"

He smiled. "Not a one. Not even one."

She grinned even more widely before turning back to Cassie. "I have my cell phone and the high heels on these shoes are weapons in and of themselves. I'll be fine."

Cassie felt indecisive. "Well..."

Robyn rolled her eyes, then gave her a wicked look—her only warning—before planting a wet one on Cassie's cheek.

Cassie froze, eyes bugging. Thought she heard Nick give a quiet little "Yes!" Then, through a haze, she heard Robyn giggling all the way to the door.

"I think she's completely lost it. Completely."

"Nah." Nick was still chuckling. "I think I scared her straight, if you want the truth."

Cassie stirred enough to give him a dirty look. "She was faking it, you perv. Get a life."

"I'm trying, I'm trying." He held up a hand.

She gazed at the door, already closed after Robyn. "I just hope she's careful."

"She will be. Relax. Honestly, it's you I'm worried about now."

She turned, frowning at the look of mock concern on his face. "What do you mean?"

He shook his head. "I'm just wondering over this change in you. Exactly when did you decide to take a walk on the wild side? *Sweetheart?*"

"Wild?" She was baffled for the briefest moment, still worrying a little about Robyn's rendezvous with a strange man. Then, catching his meaning, she scrunched her eyes shut and groaned. The past few minutes replayed for her, merciless in every detail, the charade even more outrageous in recall than it had been in real time. "I swear to God I had no idea she was going to try that."

"What? Make a move on you?"

When Cassie winced, he gave in to his own threatening chuckles. "Oh, Cass. I wish you could have seen your face. That was just priceless."

Slitting her eyes only slightly open, Cassie managed a small, painful smile. "Oh, God. I'll bet. And I hate to say it, but…thank you for calling her bluff. That was edgier than I ever want to go."

He grinned. "It really just kills you to admit it, though, doesn't it?"

She gave him a sour look. "I bet it kills you more that Robyn caved as early as she did."

"Yeah. I was sure she'd take it just a little further." He shook his head, his expression almost nostalgic. "Lips, maybe even some tongue action, would have been *cool*."

Cassie cringed. "You are so twisted, I can't even begin to tell you."

"So what would you have done if she'd—"

Cassie held up a hand. "And we are dropping that subject immediately. I need nothing more than I need a drink. *Right* now. Get me one and I'll forgive you almost anything."

He laughed some more. "Coming right up."

"Thank you." She gave him a look of grudging gratitude before he strode toward the bar. Then, thinking about Robyn and her mystery man, Cassie turned back to survey the room. Gradually she focused on her own surroundings, realizing the three guys—Robyn's puppy conquests—had now transferred their attention to her. She thought she saw money exchange hands, before one of them casually walked up to her. It was the stocky brunette she'd been chatting with before Robyn flaked.

"Hi." He offered a friendly grin.

Cassie braced, felt really, really stupid. "Um, hi. Look, about what you heard—"

"Yeah, about that." He gave her an intrigued look. "Look, I've got five bucks that says you and your girlfriend are into the whole pillow fight thing, too. So, what do you—"

Cassie groaned and pushed her way past him.

"Hey, do you want me to come by and wash your car? Clean your apartment? Make your bed?" he called after her in faint hope.

Cassie ignored him, eyes focused only on Nick. "Robyn, you are so dead."

Nick wove through the crowd, gripping a long-neck in each hand, and offered her one when he caught up to her. "Michelob, right?"

Cassie blinked. "Right. Thanks."

"So. At last."

Cassie groaned. "Why am I suddenly worried?"

He chuckled. "Are you so far out of your comfort zone? I just meant *At last*, I have you to myself. *At last*, Robyn has publicly scorned me so you can no longer thrust her in my path. She doesn't want me. *At last, at last*, I have you all to myself. And I believe she claimed your car keys on the way out?"

"My—" She dug through her purse. "Why that little sneak. How'd she do that?"

He grinned, his eyes wide and innocent.

"*You.*"

He shrugged. "Nimble fingers."

She vaguely recalled him resting a hand on her shoulder and then her arm, in the guise of comfort, while she spoke to Robyn. "And you shook her hand. That's when you passed them to her. Why, you lowdown sneak of a pickpocket."

"Only for recreation, not gain." His waggling brows gave her some indication of the recreation he meant. Adult entertainment, no doubt.

She sighed, surrendering to the inevitable. Robyn had her keys. Big deal. She might even need them. "Fine. At least she only has my car keys. I keep my apartment key on a different chain." She murmured it, surprising a disappointed look on his face. She gave him a stern look, trying to squash any other hopes he might be entertaining. "So…does that mean I can catch a ride with you?"

"Sure." He glanced around and she followed his gaze, aware that several sets of eyes still rested on her with lurid curiosity. "We can even leave now, if that's what you want. We're a bit of a spectacle still. Up to you."

She sighed. "Now's great."

He set his drink and hers on a table and motioned her onward. As he was about to follow, a hand on the arm stopped him.

Realizing at once that he'd halted, Cassie stopped

and looked back. Recognizing five-dollar man, she groaned. The nightmare would never end. She decided to let Nick handle it this time.

Probably a mistake.

"You are one hell of a lucky man." Five-dollar man spoke in a hushed voice, his eyes rounded with awe. "I mean, you know she and her friend Robyn...wow. That's way cool."

"Yeah, I know." Nick placed a humble hand over his chest. "I tell you, I'm grateful for every moment with them—I mean, *her*. It's— *Ooompf.*"

Cassie removed her pointy elbow from Nick's solar plexus, smiled sweetly at five-dollar man and stalked out the door.

"You know, that really wasn't nice." Rubbing his abdomen while he followed on her heels, Nick spoke in an injured tone that trembled slightly with mirth.

She glared over her shoulder and continued down the sidewalk.

"Hey, it's not every day that a guy is idolized by a roomful of other males. You could have at least let me savor the moment."

She rolled her eyes. "Like you need any more adulation, Mr. Cowboy in the Sky. Especially when it comes at my expense."

"At your expense? *Oh*, no. You've got it all wrong. Really! Right now, they consider you a goddess. Everything that's wonderful and mysterious about womankind. You walk on water, run with the wolves, glide with the wind—"

"Not to mention what they think I do with Robyn?"

He grinned. "Well, that's the second best part of the whole deal."

"I can only imagine the first."

He shrugged. "And you'd probably be right. We men are simple creatures."

"With twisted desires."

"Aw, lighten up, Cassie. They're just fantasies. We don't actually expect them to come true. But if there's the slightest hope..." He shook his head, his eyes momentarily dreamy.

Cassie snorted.

"What? Don't you have fantasies? Don't even try to feed me that kind of bull, Cassandra Smythe. I've held you in my arms. I *know* you have fantasies."

She halted in her tracks and turned a glare on him. "And I suppose you think you *star* in all of these supposed fantasies?"

He met her glare with a sincere, thoughtful look, verging on wistful. "Well...yeah. But probably only in my *favorite* fantasies." He paused, studying her face. "Late at night, alone...a grown man tends to dream about a woman, not an anonymous act. And I can't get you out of my head. Laughing, scheming, insulting me, worrying about the people you care about... And I can't help but imagine what making love to you would be like."

Cassie gulped. *Phenomenal.* It would be absolutely phenomenal if the experience lived up to even half of her own fantasies. No doubt about it. Oh. *No.*

He moved closer. "It's going to happen, Cass. You and me. You can't deny it. Why not now? Robyn's brave enough to take a chance. Why don't you? Ever heard of a leap of faith? Leap with me, Cassie." He was so close he breathed the words against her temple, nuzzling the tender skin.

"A leap of faith."

"Yeah." He whispered it, dipping his head. "Just imagine the possibilities." He took a tiny little bite out of her neck. The sting of pleasure arrowed straight to her belly and she couldn't catch a breath.

A door opened and a small group poured out, laughing uproariously, until somebody spoke sharply and they quieted. Cassie glanced up, dazed, and realized they were watching her and Nick.

"Let's get out of here." Nick murmured it, then took her hand. They hurried to get in his Jeep and he swiftly backed it out, whipped it around the corner and onto the main road. Cassie barely registered where they were going, just that they were going there quickly. When he parked, she was unsurprised to find that they were in front of an apartment building—and that it wasn't hers.

"Cass?"

Her breathing was shallow, her heart wavering between two opposing desires. Safety and pleasure. Safety and pleasure. She'd had safety.

Now she wanted pleasure. She turned to Nick. "Yes." She whispered it hoarsely.

He was out like a shot and she found herself tugged through the lobby door up the stairs, and through another door before she could do more than laugh breathlessly. The door slammed shut and he kissed the laughter into groans and sighs of pleasure. Cassie melted against the door, her knees failing her.

He chuckled. "Just what I wanted."

"Mmm?"

"I've dreamed of making your knees weak. For me." He whispered it, his voice raspy, sexy.

"It's working." She barely choked the words out as his lips found hers again.

She slid her arms around his neck, just as he swept her legs out from beneath her, swooping her up like some larger-than-life hero. Like the cowboy with a romantic reputation that spanned the metro area, possibly farther.

But he was hers tonight. Could that be enough?

She felt a lurch as he braced a knee on his bed, then lowered her to it. He followed her down, slowly, evenly, lowering his weight onto her body. It felt so good she could have whimpered from the pleasure.

It would have to be enough, because no way on earth could she stop him now. It just wasn't in her.

Soon, he was kissing away her doubts again and the clothes just seemed to melt away. Maybe it was those nimble pickpocket fingers or maybe she was just too blasted horny to think straight, but she was naked and happy to be so inside of mere seconds. Maybe hours. Who could tell?

Nick managed to kick his own jeans and shorts off, and soon they were skin to skin. A lovely feeling, better than familiar. Better than she'd dreamed.

Cassie smiled against his mouth, her own lips feeling swollen and still hungry. "You're right."

"I am?" He murmured it against her neck as he caressed her breast.

"Yeah." She whispered low. "You've starred in way too many of my fantasies. This is a favorite."

He stopped what he was doing and looked up. "Really? This was a fantasy?"

"I know it's stupid, but you, naked, is almost more fantasy than any sane woman needs." She inhaled and let it out slow. "There are times, Nick, when I wish I'd gone through with it and made love to you seven years ago. At least that way, the fantasy would have been complete. I'd know how it ended."

"That was your fantasy? That we'd actually...? And still now?"

She hesitated, then nodded. "I still think about it. Even before seeing you again at Becky's party. You've always been a fantasy, Nick."

His eyes flared and he took her mouth with his own, his kisses voracious, wild. His need had overcome finesse, and somehow, that was even more exciting to Cassie. He was wild for her and she couldn't help herself. She returned his kiss with every ounce of passion she'd felt then and now.

"Oh, Cass— I've never— Damn, I'm going to bust. I—"

"It's okay. Just—"

He rolled a condom on, his hands shaking. "I've wanted you. Then, now. It's worse now."

"Really?" Cassie searched his eyes. Rich, dark chocolate, melting. Melting every resolve, every inhibition, every last bit of hesitation she might have had. "I want you. Now."

"You got it." In a smooth thrust, Nick sunk himself to the hilt and Cassie groaned, her body shuddering with pleasure. It probably wouldn't even take much at all tonight, she was so turned on by his words and—

Nick groaned harshly, his thrusting increasing in pace and intensity. When he halted suddenly, she saw perspiration beading his forehead. "Oh, Cass— I think— I can't—wait—"

# _____Step 10_____

*Booty Call Blues*
*We take inventory and admit we screwed up royally.*

STILL SHUDDERING from his release, Nick dropped his face into the curve of her neck. After a shaky breath or two, he rolled to the side to relieve her of his weight. He was utterly humiliated. "Cassie. Honey. I'm sorry. You didn't—" He shook his head, at a loss. So much for his vaunted technique. What the hell had happened?

He could say, with modesty, that he'd satisfied more than his fair share of women. And it was ladies first, every time. But not Cassie. As soon as she'd started talking about her fantasies—and his part in them—his usually praiseworthy control had flown straight to hell.

Why? Why now and why her? He couldn't remember another woman's pleasure mattering to him quite this much. He couldn't remember another *woman* mattering to him quite this much.

Cassie sat up, dragging the sheet with her as she swung her legs off the bed. "No big deal."

*Shit*. Yes, it was. Cassie was barely even here with him anymore. She'd wandered somewhere deep in that head of hers. "Yeah, it is a big deal. I wanted this to be— Hell, it *will* be." He sat up, determined now. He'd taken the edge off. He wasn't so desperate for her now. He could linger over that sweet body for hours and drive the woman wild. He'd make sure she came twice. Three times. Four. Before he lost it again.

Cassie slipped off the bed before he could reach her. "No. Really. That's okay. It happens like that sometimes. Right?" She tried a smile but didn't meet his eyes.

He frowned. "But not with us."

"Well..." She glanced back at the bed, wincing just a little.

Nick stood up, too, growing more and more determined. He would make this right. "Come on, Cassie. You know lovemaking amounts to more than what happened right here, right now. I'm sorry about that, but I swear I can make it good for you. And you believe it, too, or you wouldn't be here in the first place."

She flushed a little, pulling the sheet tighter. "Maybe, maybe not. It's not really an issue now, is it? We already...and it...anyway, it's over. I want to get dressed and go home." She turned to go, but he caught her arm.

When her chin went up and she seemed to retreat a little, he let go of her arm but continued to hold her gaze. "Cass, it's not over. Don't even think that. We're just beginning. You only just decided to give it a chance. Can't you see that? We're just getting started."

"Getting started to do what? You and I both know there's no future in this. So let's just get past what happened and put it out of our minds."

"No future." He studied her. "You really believe

that. Hell, you came into this with that mind-set. What's going on?"

"Oh, Nick." She smiled ruefully at him. "This was just going to be a fling anyway. It didn't work. No big deal, right?"

"A fling."

"Yes." She twisted her lips slightly. "And the fling was with the wrong woman anyway, but I guess that can't be helped—"

"Wrong woman. You mean *Robyn?*"

"Well, yeah."

"Come on, Cassie. It's long past time to give up on anything happening between Robyn and me. I like Robyn well enough and I could see her as a friend, but I'm interested in you. It's you I want so bad it hurts. Not her."

"Well, we weren't planning a shotgun wedding between you two. Robyn's attractive, you're attractive and I thought that's all it would take." Cassie gave him an exasperated look and tugged the sheet closer.

Still twisting at the sheet and wishing it were more substantial—the better to hide from Nick's determined eyes—Cassie had to fight to keep her voice and gaze even. But her frustration was getting the best of her and humiliation was catching up fast. This was a truly stupid conversation to be having, right here, right now, with this man—no matter how disappointing the sex had been. Especially now that she realized she could never handle the idea of him and Robyn together, anyway.

God, she just wanted to cry. When she thought of all

the times she'd fantasized about this and now compared those fantasies to reality...it shot a girl's dreams straight to hell. She should have known this was all a mistake. So much for her sign. So much for there being some special reason why he kept pursuing her. Fate. Ha. Destiny, ha. She'd just blinded herself to reality all over again. What's worse, she was very much afraid that disappointing sex or no, she was hooked on Nick all over again.

"Wait a minute." Nick was frowning. "Fling. You specifically said fling. This really wasn't your typical setup. You weren't trying to set Robyn and me up for real. You were specifically trying to involve us in a *fling*. What the hell for?"

Cassie groaned. "Look. You were just supposed to help her get over her ex. I know you're not into permanent relationships, so I thought you'd be the perfect, well, temporary man, for her."

"Temporary man? What the hell is that? At the end of the fling, poof, I turn into a damned *pumpkin?*"

"Nick, you know what I meant." Cassie worked to keep her voice even. She hadn't realized he'd go off the deep end over this. "We just meant...a brief, cheerful little romance. Instead of picket fences and happily-ever-after. We just figured that you'd be...up...for that kind of thing...as opposed to..." Her voice trailed off. Cassie cringed a little. Okay, so that didn't sound so good when described in those terms—

"God, Cassie. Where do you get off, making my decisions for me? All based on what you knew about me seven years ago. Believe it or not, a lot of guys grow up after college. We become big boys then and don't need a different piece of candy every five minutes."

*Ouch. Okay, he was pissed.* "Look, I'm sorry if I misjudged you. I didn't mean any harm—"

"*If?* You still don't get it, do you?"

"Look, it's a moot point. I give up on matchmaking between you and Robyn. Satisfied?"

"Not nearly."

"Fine. So you're trying to convince me that you're through with playing the field. With flings. With playing the temporary man. That you're sincerely interested in forming a real relationship with a woman." It was a direct challenge and a doozy at that. How she wished he could answer to it. Despite the reality.

"And what if I am?"

"Really. So tell me this, then, *Cowboy.* Why do you still lug that reputation of yours all over the place? In your personal life, in your professional life?"

He shrugged, his frustration obviously getting the better of him. "I don't *know.* I swear to God, I don't know. I've been trying to ditch the damn thing for years now, but I think it would destroy Chad and Jerry to admit the truth. That this stupid reputation's been overblown for years now."

She paused, staring at him. "You're serious."

"Yes, I'm serious. Nobody believes it, but I'm serious."

"Really? So any rumors, innuendo…it's all just a misunderstanding? Because of your friends bragging on you?" She studied him, eyes narrowed.

"If the incident in question was dated any later than

six years ago and involved any but one or two women I was seeing casually, you'd better believe it. My social life, as much as I hate to admit it, has pretty much tanked in favor of my business." He threw his hands up. "Hell, you know how hard it is to start a business on your own. Worry and sweat and eighty-hour weeks. Sort of kills the drive for romance, you know?"

She smiled wryly. "You could say that, yeah."

He pressed further. "Given those eighty-hour weeks, Cass, tell me where the hell I would find time to do as many women as the guys claim I do. I would be dead."

She chuckled just a little. "Takes a big man to admit it."

"No. Just one who's being honest and who desperately wants a real chance with you. Please? Let me fix this." He glanced at the bed. "I can. We deserve this."

She stole a quick look at the bed, too, her feelings wavering between appalled and intrigued. "Just like that? You think we can just logic our way back into the sack and into sex? Gee, that'll guarantee me an orgasm."

He stepped forward, purposeful. "No, but *I* would."

Her eyes widened and she retreated a step. "Whoa, boy. Take it down a notch. I mean, sometimes these things just happen. And sometimes they happen for a reason. It could be that you and I just aren't meant to be. You know?" She tried a shaky smile as he continued his slow approach. Truly, her heart was aching, and if he got any closer—

"No, I *don't* know."

"Sure you do. Serendipity. Luck. Fate. What happens will happen, no need to force matters...."

"So you're saying what happened just now in this bed means something more than that you turned me on so bad I couldn't wait this first time? I don't think so. I think I was just getting started. And now I'd like to do it right." He raised an eyebrow and looked down at her, just a breath away from him now. "So what do you say?"

She wavered, feeling her own frustrated desire still gnawing at her. And her hopes. It was tempting, so tempting, to give the man another chance. Maybe—

No. That one taste, as brief and unsatisfactory as it was, was more delicious, more addicting than she could handle. She would not get her heart broken by one Nick Ranger a second time in this lifetime. A modern-day Casanova seeking reform and relationship. Gee, sounded like a sure thing. Or not. *Damn* it. Her stomach knotting with wishes and regrets, she shook her head and tried for a low, even tone that didn't challenge. "I'm sorry, Nick, but—"

Nick touched a finger to her lips, halting her words.

She glanced up, startled, to see the intensity in his eyes. "Don't say it, Cass. Please. Whatever you say, just don't make it no. Make it maybe. Or another time. Or tomorrow. Or now. Just not *no*."

She studied him, curious, shaken, and perhaps even a little awed as he brushed the finger over her lips before dropping it away. She barely refrained from licking where he'd touched and cleared her throat. "I... It really means that much to you? A second chance?"

She was weakening. Despite every bit of common sense, despite her mother's experiences and lectures on the subject of men with itchy feet, despite everything Cassie herself wanted out of life. Nick just wasn't the kind of guy to figure into a girl's destiny. Nothing responsible or forever-after about him. Another distraction. Another blind spot.

"Yeah. It means that much to me."

"Because of your reputation or—"

"To hell with my reputation. This is just you and me."

She clutched the sheet tightly for a moment, staring at the wall behind him. She nibbled at her lower lip, still swollen and sensitive from his kisses.

"What do you say, Cass?"

"I say..." She glanced up at him then quickly away, her breathing unsteady and her resolve as stiff as jelly. "Maybe. A really conditional maybe."

"Fine. Okay. I can do maybe. As long as I'm given a chance to turn that maybe into a yes."

Feeling increasingly naked in her sheet—and finding it hard to keep her own gaze from the more intimate portions of Nick in all his naked glory—Cassie backed discreetly away. "I'm going to get dressed now."

Sighing his reluctance, Nick rubbed a hand roughly down his face, then shrugged and nodded. "Okay. I'll take you home."

Ignoring the dimmed light of disappointment in his eyes, Cassie dipped quickly to snag her dress and underwear off the floor, then scooted into the bathroom. She closed the door behind her.

Outside the bathroom, Nick disposed of the condom, then grimly yanked his jeans on, leg by leg. He buttoned the fly and shrugged into a shirt, yanking it into place hard enough that he heard the material rip a little. He felt like punching something. He'd come so close—and then screwed up so badly. Given what he'd seen of Cassie's quirky adherence to the fate principle—which he was more likely to ascribe to indecisiveness—he should have known his butt was riding on his performance tonight. Naturally, he'd bombed out completely.

Still, he'd managed to talk her out of a complete rejection of him. Things were still iffy, but with some care, he'd have a second opportunity. And this time he'd ensure that Cassie was so exhausted with pleasure that she'd consider occupying a permanent place in his bed and in his life.

ON THE SHORT DRIVE back to her apartment, Cassie felt her own tension creeping higher. She felt tugged in two opposing directions and it sucked. Her hormones wailed that she should give Nick another chance. She was quite aware—every nerve ending in her body was quite aware—that he could launch her into the stratosphere with just a few standard maneuvers.

Her whirling emotions, however, rendered her too vulnerable to surrender to such a delight. Once Nick launched her poor, quivering body into orbit, she very much feared she'd be there for the duration. Nick could—and very possibly *would*—break her heart.

No, sex wasn't the be-all, end-all of the world and she was pretty sure that wasn't a real problem for Nick. He'd probably abstained for a while and found himself trigger-happy before they even got to his apartment. No doubt the second round would have been glorious.

Unfortunately, love—true, *lasting* love, the be-all, end-all of *her* world—could likely also factor into the situation. Oh, but she could fall for him and hard. Assuming he fell, too, and just as hard, she could be rapturously happy, just by giving in to the longings of those raging hormones and her heart. But if he didn't...

At least she'd bought some time to make her decision. She hadn't quite ended things between her and Nick, but she also hadn't promised him anything. Surely, soon, she'd have a sign either way what she should do. A girl could always hope. But she'd need an obvious sign. No more of this uncertain reading between the lines and seeking excuses and reasons. That only bought her trouble and more diversions.

So what could it be? What kind of sign would she be looking for? A brick slamming into her head? Propelled by a slingshot made out of Nick's Jockeys, perhaps?

Her lips twisted reluctantly at that image. That would do it. Yeah, a girl could always hope.

THE SIGN, AS IT TURNED OUT, huddled pathetically in the hallway outside Cassie's apartment door.

"Robyn?" Ignoring Nick, Cassie rushed over and gently helped Robyn to her feet.

"Oh, Cass." Throwing her arms around Cassie's neck, Robyn buried her face into Cass's shoulder. "I'm sorry. I couldn't go home, not even to get the key to your apartment so I could let myself in. He'd find me there and—"

"What?" Freshly alarmed, Cassie set Robyn back from her so she could survey for damage. "Are you hurt? Did that guy hurt you?"

Nick stepped forward, careful to still keep a courteous distance. "Do we need an ambulance? The police? I can make the call."

Robyn was already shaking her head, burying it in Cassie's shoulder to hide from Nick.

Cassie was unconvinced. She'd seen the wounded look in her friend's eyes. "Ooooh. That slime. Just let me get my hands on Man As Island, and he'll see his damn *island* make like Atlantis and *sink*."

"It's okay, Cass. I'm okay. Mostly. He didn't hurt me. Not like that."

"Then what? What happened?"

Robyn raised her head from Cassie's shoulder and painfully met her friend's eyes. "Man As Island...well, he's Alex, Cassie. *Alex*. I've been corresponding with Alex all this time. And he knew. I didn't."

Cassie stared, her mind still catching up to make the connection. Alex...Robyn's ex...the guy who— "You're kidding me." The connection formed, the implications settling where they must. "You mean, after insulting you over and over again into dumping him, then not even accepting that he was dumped...now he's skulking around on the Internet, using an alias, lying to you... Was he...stalking you? Is this what this is about?"

Robyn was already shaking her head, tears forming in her eyes. "No. I actually liked corresponding with...Man As Island...I encouraged it, even. We didn't exchange real names or anything because...well, I kind of liked the mystery. I thought we both did. But that was when I didn't know who he really was. I should have realized...the information he didn't offer...other stuff. What an idiot I was. So much for romance and mystery and taking a chance on either."

"But he knew it was you. How did it all start up, then? How did he make the connection?"

Robyn shrugged. "I don't know. He swore to me that he didn't know it was me at first. That he was just looking for someone to talk to. Someone who didn't know him. And then I guess I revealed enough that he figured out who I was. But then he didn't bother to let me in on the secret. God, I feel violated. Like he invaded my privacy and my thoughts...."

"That's because he did. There must be something we can do to him."

"I already did." Robyn looked mutinous suddenly. "He'll be singing soprano for a little while."

At a distinctly masculine wince behind them, both women looked up. Cassie met Nick's eyes, then looked away. Another door down the hallway opened up, a head peeked out then popped back inside, and the door closed.

"Maybe we should take this inside?" Nick murmured the suggestion.

"You're probably right." Cassie dug in her purse for her key. Once she got the door unlocked, Cassie gently guided Robyn past, then turned to face Nick, discreetly barring his entry. She met his eyes briefly, then looked away.

"I see." He spoke low. "So do you just want privacy or have I suddenly rejoined the ranks of enemy?"

"Oh, Nick." She sighed. "You're not the enemy, but—" She glanced back at Robyn, who was standing at the window, staring sightlessly outside.

"But there's Robyn. Again." He raised an eyebrow. "I hate to point out the obvious, but not only did she reject me earlier in favor of her online friend, but she's also still hung up on her boyfriend. Even if tonight hadn't happened, I don't think your matchmaking efforts between Robyn and me would have worked out."

She shook her head. "I know, I know. And, that's not what I meant. I realize that's not going to happen. But Robyn needs me right now and—"

"And this is your way of kissing me off anyway. You're just using Robyn as an excuse. Again. Why don't you at least admit it, Cassie? At least do me that courtesy."

She pursed her lips. "I'm sorry, Nick. I just don't think it would work out for us. We're not—"

He reached in with both hands, cupped her shoulders and lifted her to her toes for a hard, intent-filled kiss. He was merciless and skilled and...successful.

Set free at last, Cassie swayed into the doorjamb and just stared up at him, her lips hot and still hungry.

His eyes glittered with the same hunger, but he spoke quietly. "You're wrong." He glanced past her at Robyn, who'd turned to stare at them, then met her eyes again. "Come on, Cassie. Yeah, I screwed up, but you and I know I could have fixed it. I still can. Just give me an honest-to-God chance and you'll see." He spoke in a low, heated whisper.

When she started to turn away, he stopped her with his words. "Remember flying with me on my plane?"

She looked up and nodded reluctantly. How could she ever forget?

"I was the one flying that plane and you trusted me to keep you safe. You were scared as hell, but it was worth every minute of it. Wasn't it? Trust me again. Take the risk. I guarantee you won't regret it." Touching her lips with a finger, he gave her a last, compelling look, then turned and strode down the hallway.

A few minutes later Cassie felt a hand on her shoulder and jumped. She realized she was still standing with the door open, staring at a now-empty hallway.

"You and Nick?" Robyn spoke in a voice that was hoarse with her earlier emotion, but the concern still showed.

Cassie nodded, trying to catch a breath past the tightness in her chest. "But that's not...important, really. Alex. Tell me more. What happened?"

Robyn's throat worked. "Well, I waited at the bar for a few minutes, but no one showed up. That's when the bartender passed me a note, suggesting I meet Man As Island outside by the lamp post."

That distracted her. "You went to meet him alone *outside?* What are you, *nuts?* He could have been any-one—"

"I know, I know. But the post was still within sight of the bar. People looking out the window would have seen us, so I thought it was okay."

"I disagree...but go on with your story."

She shrugged. "I saw him. We talked. We argued. It got to be quite the spectacle, though, and I wasn't through chewing him out...so we got into his car and argued some more in the parking lot."

"And?" Cassie already dreaded it.

"We made out. Like we always did after a fight."

Cassie groaned. "And then?"

"He just assumed everything was okay. In his high-handed way. That I was going to go back to his apartment and we'd have sex and continue on as though nothing else had ever happened. So I got mad again, and accidentally—I really didn't mean to, believe it or not—kneed him...*there*. I was just trying to get off of him, and—" Robyn shook her head. "Anyway, I adjusted my clothes, got out, ran to my own car—well, *your* car." She gave Cassie a guilty look. "And here I am."

Ignoring the car reference as unimportant, given larger events, Cassie groaned again. "So, basically, you fell off the wagon?"

Robyn laughed and it sounded like a sob. "You could say that. Although, it didn't go as far as it could have."

Cassie gave a rueful, totally unamused chuckle and dropped her forehead against the door. "Wow. We're quite a pair."

"Why do you say that?"

Still leaning against the door, Cassie turned her head to give Robyn a pointed, painful look.

Robyn raised her eyebrows. "You and Nick?"

Cassie grimaced. "You could say that. I wish I'd had a little of your restraint...."

"You mean you—" Robyn's eyes widened. "Good grief, Cass, why didn't you say so?" Robyn tugged her to the couch. "We get caught up in my dramas all the time. You know, you're allowed to tell me to shut up when you have one of your own."

"Wasn't all that dramatic, if you want the truth."

"But you two...had sex?"

Cassie shrugged and nodded. "It just wasn't exactly how I imagined it."

"What do you mean?"

"I guess you could say our cowboy in the sky...fell off the horse in bed."

Robyn's jaw dropped open. *He couldn't get it up?*

"No, it went up okay. It just had a good time and left me stranded is all."

Robyn winced.

"Yeah." Cassie reflected wistfully. "I really had high hopes." Dreams, fantasies...the faintest whispers of love in her fickle, idiotic heart. Not smart.

"What a bummer." Robyn gave her a sympathetic look.

"Yeah."

"But at least you know, right?"

"So you think I should...give up on him? Based on this? I mean, it was our first time together. Things were bound to be...you know." She sighed, wavering again. She wanted him. She really, really did. Even despite what had happened. Or maybe even—and she knew this was contrary as hell—*because* of what had happened. Nick was more than she'd assumed. Smart, funny, sensitive even, despite the reputation. And she was pretty sure, given the chance, that he'd—

"Well, no. Not based *just* on this." Robyn frowned. "I'd say this is just the indicator, the last straw, the brick falling on your head. The wake-up call before you repeat past mistakes. I mean, there's all the other stuff, remember? The reasons you've kept away from him until now?"

Cassie shrugged.

Robyn looked alarmed. "Come on, Cass. I've heard this speech from you so often I know it by heart." She closed her eyes, hand laid across her heart and spoke in a singsong voice as though reciting. "If the man can't commit, then the man can't commit. And no matter how much you love him, you can't force or persuade him to act contrary to his basic nature. Even if it works temporarily, it will only backfire on you in the end. Furniture and property are fixer-uppers, not men." Robyn opened her eyes and continued even more emphatically. "Men are strictly *take them as they are*. Remember? Any of this ringing a bell? Hello?"

Well, Cassie supposed the positive thing was that Robyn really had been listening during all those lectures she'd read her. Would Robyn follow the advice, too? Cass glanced around. No Alex in sight. Well, if Robyn could choose the smarter path, Cassie supposed the least she could do was listen to her own words of so-called wisdom. "I remember. You're right." She shook her head. "Maybe women like you and me should travel only in pairs. Obviously, we're not trustworthy on our own around men."

Robyn gave her a sickly grin. "Heck, we could even give the lesbian thing a shot."

Cassie gave her a droll look and, through tear-filled eyes, she spoke without inflection. "Ooh, baby. You turn me on."

Robyn cracked up for real. "Oh, Cass, I do love you. In a totally platonic, *entirely heterosexual* type of way."

Cassie grinned ruefully, wiping the heel of her hand across drippy eyes. "Me, too."

# Step 11

*Temporary Celibacy*
*Through frustration and insanity, we seek*
*a better understanding of our loves and lives.*

"OH, GOD. JUST ONE MORE rep and I will die. I swear it."
Cassie groaned through her sweat and misery, staring
up at the damn dumbbell. Damnbell. Yeah, there was a
better name for it. *Damn*bell.

Damnbell, damnbell, damnbell. And, gee, there was
an apt name for an idiot like herself, too. Missing a footloose guy like Nick so bad she took to the gym to sweat
out her frustration. Sexual and otherwise.

It had been almost two weeks since she'd seen him
last. She'd ignored his phone calls, refused to answer
the door, responded only to business-related e-mails.
She'd already sent him an invoice with a professional-
sounding little note offering him three months of online
assistance and maintenance...in lieu of private Web site
lessons. It was cold but necessary.

And, every night since that last encounter, she'd
dreamed a more satisfying ending to their lovemaking.
She was obsessed with him all over again. If she were
honest with herself, she'd admit she'd fallen for those
dark chocolate eyes and even harder than before. She

was hooked. It was killing her. She couldn't handle it, so lessons were out. She couldn't see him, even professionally. Not if she had to swear off of him all over again. Distance was best.

Until two days ago she'd had work climbing all over her to keep her mind busy and off Nick. She'd been putting in sixteen-hour-plus days, just to catch up on stuff she'd let go. And to get a jump on projects she was starting. Now, horror of horrors, she'd actually worked herself into free time.

Which she was currently wasting on damnbells in this damn gym. Staring up at the bar, she suppressed another whimper and closed her eyes.

And, yep, she'd been right all along. Everything really did get complicated when you slept with a guy and money changed hands. Even if the money and sex were totally unrelated. Very bad move.

Groaning, she tightened her hands on the dumbbell bar again, really tried to work up the strength and initiative to lift the damn thing just one more time. One more lift and she'd complete the damn set and head to the showers.

"Why, it's Cas-*san*-dra."

At the obvious delight in the too obvious woman's voice, Cassie couldn't decide whether to launch the damnbell at the cheerleader or to whimper in defeat. "Hi, Becky."

Becky sat her svelte self down on a bench next to Cassie. A thong leotard. What was the practical purpose of a thong leotard? Fashion that flossed while you perspired and expired. Cassie chafed just thinking about it.

"I almost never see you here." Becky spoke with affectionate condescension. "Robyn's here all the time, it seems, but never you."

Sexual frustration. Made sense. Great minds think alike.

Becky burbled on happily. "Are you making good on an old New Year's resolution?"

"Sure. Why not? A girl is nothing without her resolutions, right?" Cassie stared grimly at the damnbell bar she still clutched. Just one more. But Becky would see her arms trembling with strain even if she somehow managed to keep the thing from smashing down on her own boobs.

"Oh, I think resolutions are just lovely, but sometimes we're a little hasty making them. We're not always realistic." Becky stood up and, amazingly, adjusted Cassie's grip on the bar. "There. If you lift correctly, there's less chance of hurting yourself."

Cassie stared, then mumbled, "Thanks."

"How many more do you have? I saw you doing several before...so it can't be many. Don't overdo. I'll spot you."

"One more...set of eight." *I'm an idiot. A vain, self-destructive idiot.* She inhaled and held it before shoving the damn thing up again.

"Exhale on the exertion...." Becky murmured, watchful.

"Right." Cassie grunted through another rep.

Amazingly she got through the extra set, but then just sagged in place, completely ditching her pride and any pretense. "I never work out."

Becky laughed. "I know. Still...if you hope to keep your shape and attract male attention..." She smoothed a hand over a sleek hip. "It's well worth it."

Cassie closed her eyes, restraining the urge. Becky had actually been kind, so Cassie could find it in her bruised heart to forgive a flub or two—

"Like Nick, for example, is well worth holding on to, if you can." She smiled thoughtfully at Cassie. "He has quite the wandering eye, but it did rest—at least momentarily—on you."

*And?*

"For example, Shannon's here all the time and she looks great. Have you met Shannon? Nick brought her to my parties a few times. I just saw them together again the other night. They were at a little Italian place near here." She smiled. "They seemed to be enjoying themselves immensely. Especially for being in such a public place."

"That's nice." Cassie wrenched her beleaguered body into an upright position and stalked off toward the treadmill. Lovely. While she'd been eating her heart out over Nick, he'd been romancing *Shannon* in between sincerely felt phone messages and electronic pleas to *Cassie*. Jerk.

And now, as much as she hated to admit it, her heart ached worse than her biceps and pectorals did. Perhaps more physical pain would distract her.

"Eeeeewww. Aren't you going to wipe that off? Gym etiquette, you know." Becky paused. "Wow. You'd better drink some water, too."

Cursing under her breath, Cassie swiped a towel

over the perspiration-slick bench. When Becky moved with every intention of following Cassie to the treadmill, Cassie changed her mind and escaped to the locker room. Treadmill she would conquer tomorrow. And possibly the heartache, as well—if she could manage to erase the mental picture of Nick and the curvy Shannon enjoying each other. It was going to take a lot of treadmill time. Probably more than she had at her disposal.

"HAVE YOU TALKED TO HIM? Since that night?" Robyn continued filing her toenails. It was Friday night—a full three weeks since the sports class and all the foolishness that had ensued. Tonight Robyn had declared an embargo on the opposite sex, then invited herself over for a girls' makeover session. The theory was that, if they felt hot and well put-together, they would be. Men or no men.

Cassie squinted at her little toe, carefully swiping a coat of clear base on the nail. Maybe her eyesight was going. Everything was blurry....

"Cass?"

"Hmm?" Blinking rapidly, she realized the blur was a film of tears. She was an emotional wreck. So much for the curative powers of beauty treatments. She faked a lopsided grimace and wiped her eyes on her T-shirt, as though she had something in her eye.

"Have you talked to Nick?"

"No. Not since that night. I did send an invoice and a note, like we discussed. So...I guess you could say I have no reason to talk to him in person anymore. Any further communication can be via e-mail."

Robyn stopped filing and studied her friend. "And it's still tearing you up inside."

"Maybe."

Robyn sighed. "If it helps any, I feel as wussy as you."

"Gee. I feel tons better now." Cassie gave her a lopsided grin and concentrated on the toenails of her left foot.

"Maybe we should start a support group for recovering sexaholics."

Cassie managed a laugh. "I think it's been done. Besides. If sex were the only problem, I don't think we'd be this messed up. Do you?"

"Probably not. Makes you wonder why we bother."

"With?"

"The beauty treatments, the dating, everything. I mean, neither of us is over a guy we shouldn't even be with...so what's the point? I'm not looking at anyone else because I keep thinking of Alex and you can't even take your mind off Nick long enough to paint all your toenails. You missed the middle one."

Cassie paused, frowned, then grumbled absently as she swiped a coat over the middle toenail. "I see your point. So what is this? What are we trying to do here?"

"Think. Contemplate our navels."

Cassie giggled shakily. "You can gaze all you want at your navel. Mine needs no attention from me whatsoever. We live parallel lives and prefer it that way."

"Do we? All of us? Live parallel lives?" Robyn sounded contemplative.

"Stop staring at your belly button, Robyn. You're scaring me."

"I'm serious. We're all so afraid to get involved. Except where it's safe. I consider you safe and you consider me safe, but hetero, hetero, hetero. And we each have a libido to consider."

"True enough. And..." Cassie shoved the brush back in the container and screwed it tightly. "There's nothing safe about Alex or Nick. But we want them anyway." She met Robyn's eyes. "Are we doing this wrong?"

Robyn stared into her eyes for a moment, then let her gaze drop again as she shrugged. "I don't know. I know I couldn't let Alex keep walking all over me."

"I won't argue with that. But what am I doing? I'm staying away from Nick because...I'm afraid?"

Robyn tipped her head to the side in thought. "Probably. But that's not a sure sign you should jump in, either. Fear's a healthy emotion. It keeps us from leaping off cliffs and playing in traffic. Maybe fear's keeping you from a similar catastrophe."

"Yeah..." Absently selecting a pretty fuchsia color—the brighter the color, the better to brighten the mood?—she considered further.

"You sound less than convinced." Robyn set aside the file and snagged the base polish.

Concentrating on her big toe, Cassie smiled ruefully as she swiped the brush carefully across the nail. "Could be because I'm horny."

Robyn laughed.

Cassie's smile faded. "Could be because I miss him."

"Could be...that you need to think some more about the risks you're taking? What you have to lose...and what you have to gain? Sometimes the real deal's messier than what we'd hoped, but more worthwhile than we'd dreamed."

Cassie's hand stilled and she glanced up at Robyn. "When did you get so smart, anyway?"

Robyn gave her a cheeky smile. "It just sounded good. Why, did it mean something?"

"Smartass."

Still, Robyn was square-on with her assessment. Cassie had some thinking to do. If she still couldn't forget Nick, then maybe it was worth...experimenting. A little. Could she bear it? If it failed? What if Nick really couldn't commit? What if he was sticking his toe in waters too deep for him yet and she was the one who sank?

But wasn't she sinking anyway?

Monday afternoon, Cassie still didn't have the answers to all her questions and she still didn't know anything beyond the fact that she was tired of thinking about it and racking her brain for solutions.

And now it was even interfering with her work. Nick's name mysteriously appeared over and over on a new client's home page. At this rate, she'd eventually go well beyond heartbroken to just plain flat broke.

Sighing, she hit the delete key again and arrowed to the top to reread the damned thing and check for errors. Then she closed it down and, hesitantly, pulled up Nick's site. She had some changes to make, changes he'd e-mailed to her in response to her invoice and brusque business letter.

To her disappointment, he hadn't included anything personal in the communication. And, yes, of course she realized how contrary that was. She was the one severing the personal ties. She supposed she'd just hoped he'd beg and grovel until she was compelled to break down the flimsy barriers she'd erected against him.

Sighing, she pulled up the screen and skimmed the numbers, pausing over one group in particular. These didn't add up. Could be an error...or maybe she should check with Nick?

Cassie chewed on a fingernail. She could e-mail him. Or call him, even. Certainly he wasn't online all the time. Who knew when he would check his e-mail again. If she called...

Sure, it was just an excuse to hear his voice, but what could it hurt? She was still weaning herself off of him and, if just hearing his voice helped still the urge to run and leap all over the man's bones, maybe she ought to do it.

But what if he saw through it? What if she looked like the needy idiot that she really was? Well, at least then the humiliation would keep her well away from the man. Unless he issued her an invitation she couldn't refuse.

Ugh. Then what? And still, she needed to ask him about the site. It was the responsible thing to do, right? And if he happened to ask her out, too, or if she simply enjoyed hearing his voice, it was no big deal, right?

To call or not to call. To call or...not to call. To call or...

"Oh, just pick up the phone, you wuss." She yanked the phone off the hook and dialed six numbers, pausing over the seventh. "What if it's the answering machine? What kind of message...?" She inhaled sharply, inspiration saving her. "No message. If I call and he picks up, I was meant to do this. Just hear his voice, ask my stupid question and hang up. If he doesn't pick up...I was just saved from my own stupidity and should thank my lucky stars. There. Mission accomplished. Decision made."

She stabbed the last number and waited, heart racing. "Be there. Don't be there." She wanted him to be there, but perhaps he shouldn't be—

"Hello?" The voice was a woman's.

Cassie slammed the phone down, her stomach churning. *Not* one of the options. And she still felt like an idiot. How mature.

Why couldn't life be simpler? Why couldn't the man answer or not answer his own stupid phone? Well, it had been a stupid question anyway. Still grumbling, she turned back to her computer, prepared to input the changes Nick had requested. She'd just call up his site again, make the changes without questioning them— which is what she should have done in the first place— and—

The phone rang. Cassie jumped. It rang again. She took a deep breath. *Could be a client. Act like an adult, Cass.*

"Hello?"

"Cassie? You called." It was Nick, sounding urgent and sure of his information.

"I— How did you—"

"Caller ID."

"Right." Caller ID. Just what an indecisive weenie needed in this day and age. How was a girl supposed to avoid her decisions?

"Was there something you needed from me?" He spoke low.

Oh, God, was there ever. "I— No. *Yes*. Yes, of course." She inhaled, let it out slow. "I had a question. About your Web site."

"My Web site. Right." He sounded disappointed.

"Um, yeah. Some of those numbers you e-mailed me seem off. Maybe you could confirm or change them?"

"Sure. Read them off." He sounded businesslike now.

She did so, pausing at the end, her cheeks burning. The numbers weren't off. He just offered a discount for package lessons. She knew that. Any idiot could guess that.

"Consider it confirmed. Those numbers are right." He paused. "I do appreciate you calling to check on it, though."

"I just...wanted to make sure." She trailed off, uncertainly, her heart pounding out a sickly rhythm.

"Thanks. Cassie...how are you? I've missed you."

"Nick..."

"I wanted to call you this weekend, but I thought you might hang up on me."

"I wouldn't hang up on you, Nick."

He sighed. "I know. You would've let the machine get it. Or else you'd sound...businesslike. That's almost worse."

She didn't respond. She couldn't.

"I had something I wanted to tell you." He paused, a coaxing note in his voice. "It's about the Drummonds..."

His almost-mile-high clients. She blinked, the sickly knot in her belly loosening a little. "Yeah?"

"I think I solved my problem."

"You did? How?" She gave a half laugh. "Did you offer them train tickets?"

"You know, I actually tried that, but no go. It's not convenient and not nearly as—" He swallowed audibly. "*Exciting.* And that's a direct quote, by the way."

She chuckled for real. "So what worked, then?"

"I scammed them. I told them they'd won a free flying lesson if they signed up for the discounted beginner's package. They were enthusiastic about it, so now I'm teaching Mr. Drummond how to fly."

She gasped. "Oh, my God. That's ingenious."

"I thought so." He sounded smug. "This way, he's either in pilot or co-pilot's position and his wife's out of arm's reach."

"Amazing."

"It gets better. After he gets his certification, he wants to invest in his own plane to take to and from their condo and elsewhere, but it'll be a little one. Occasionally, he'll need freight service from me. So I get to keep their business—both the lessons and the freight service—without the discomfort of taxiing their love nest back and forth."

Cassie laughed long and hard. "Oh, Nick, that is so clever. You must be thrilled."

"Thrilled, hell." He laughed. "I was so relieved that it even worked, I wanted to cry like a baby."

"I don't blame you. So no more mile-high club for you." Her chuckles dwindled as she realized what she'd said.

"Oh, Cass. For you, I'd—"

"I...have to go, Nick. I just wanted to check those numbers."

"I want to see you. When Shannon told me you'd called, I was so sure that's what you wanted, too."

*Shannon.* The woman who'd answered the phone. And, according to Becky, the woman he'd taken to dinner very recently. While he'd supposedly been pining away for Cassie. Her manner cooled. "Like I said, I was just checking the numbers."

"Cassie, Shannon was just here on business. We set up arrangements over dinner the other night—as part of her new job duties since she got promoted—and she followed up in person today. Her dad's company charters me sometimes."

"Of course."

"Cassie, don't pull this. You know I'd tell you if I was seeing her. I don't lie." He spoke quietly. "Admit at least to yourself that Shannon's just one more excuse. You don't want to take the risk. And, granted, I'm a bit of a risk. Ugly track record. And I know you don't exactly trust the planes, either. I can understand that. *But*

I think it's something you'd get past in time. The track record...the possibility of a future...well, I guess those will just take a leap of faith from you."

She didn't respond. There was nothing to argue when the man was only stating the truth as he saw it.

"Cass?" He prompted her gently. "Do you think there's any possibility...?"

She closed her eyes, then spoke quietly. Strange how talking on the phone could allow people to be intimate with each other, say things they couldn't say when they were together in person. "I don't know, Nick. I can't seem to even think clearly when the subject involves you. Maybe that's why I have such a hard time making a clear decision. And then sticking to it. Maybe that's why, with you, I'm always looking for a sign, something to tell me that what we have is right. That it stands a chance. I guess...that means you're right about me. I'm afraid of the risk."

"And you're holding out for...a sign?" He sounded baffled.

She smiled ruefully, knowing he could hear it in her voice. "It sounds stupid, but I feel like, if it's meant to be, I'll know it."

There was a pause. "You know how frustrating that is for me, don't you? I'm waiting for some supernatural event to convince you I'm worth your time."

She sighed. "Yes, I know. I'm sorry."

"But you're thinking about it. You and me. Beyond the supernatural event. Right?"

"Yes, I'm thinking about it." How could she do otherwise?

"Keep thinking about it. Just *keeeeep* thinking about it. *Don't* stop thinking about it."

She laughed a little at his deliberate mimicry of a hypnotist. "I'm not that easily swayed."

"Was worth a shot... Don't give up, Cass."

She nodded, unable to say more. To be honest, she wasn't sure she *could* give him up. Talk about hopeless.

# _____Step 12_____

_Recovery_
_Realizing that all flights of fancy are possible_
_on wings of hope, we follow our hearts and spread the love._

A WEEK AND A DAY LATER found Cassie in the middle of
what had become a regular pastime. Staring at a computer screen and seeing and comprehending absolutely
nothing. Thank God she'd been able to work like a mad-
woman that first week or two after Nick, but now...

When the doorbell rang and she saw the courier's
truck parked on the street below, Cassie was only too
relieved to be called away from her computer.

"Thanks." She smiled at the deliveryman and shut
the door, her gaze fixed on the return address scrawled
across the padded envelope. It was from Nick.

Carefully, knowing it was just business and that she
needed it to be just business anyway, she opened the
envelope. Sure enough, there was a disk inside. But
also, a note:

"Cassie,
Here's some data and that last picture I promised
you. But, please, don't look at it or load it onto the
site yet. I want you to stop by the hangar first.

There's something you need to see in person before the picture makes sense to you. I couldn't explain in a note.

Yours always,
Nick.

After skimming the note, she stared at the last few words, running a finger over them as she pondered. *Yours always...* Wouldn't it be just lovely if he meant it literally? Hers always. Now and forever. A girl could dream.

*Dream.* What was she, pathetically adolescent and spinning fairy tales again? It hadn't given her a loving, reliable father back then, and it wouldn't change things now with Nick. Feeling cynical and impatient suddenly, Cassie dropped the disk and note back into the envelope and tossed it on her desk. She raked her hands through her hair, gazing around at her sparsely furnished apartment.

Was this all she was supposed to have? A cool apartment, a job she loved but which got pretty isolating on occasion...and dreams? God knew the men weren't exactly lining up at her door. At least, no man that she really wanted. Which was fine with her and exactly the way she wanted things.

Until Nick.

*Yours always...*

Oh, God, she missed him. It was getting harder and harder to accept the idea of giving him up for good. Could she honestly play the online business associate and nothing more to him? She'd seen him naked and felt his hands on her naked body. He'd stirred her, so much more than any other man. He'd touched her body, her mind, her funny bone, her heart, her soul...

She dropped her hands and paced her apartment. Maybe...what if she...

"Oh, what a wimp." Annoyed with herself, she raked a brush through her hair and grabbed her purse. At the very least, she could go to the hangar to see what he wanted her to see. It was the adult thing to do.

Just as she reached for the doorknob, it twisted beneath her hand and swung inward, forcing Cassie back a step. She raised startled eyes to see a frantic-looking Robyn.

"Cass. I need you."

"Huh?"

"Or, rather, I need Nick. Can you help me?"

*"No."* It came out before she even thought about it. Cassie just stared a moment, then repeated it. "No. He's mine. I'm keeping." And she was. She *would*, damn it. She raised her chin. Wow, that had been easier than she thought it would be. Decision made. Love acknowledged. And Nick was her love. It was about time she told good old fate to take a hike and took control of her own destiny. It felt good. Empowering. She loved Nick and she was keeping him.

"Well, duh." Robyn blinked. "Welcome to the light." Then she waved an impatient hand. "Look, I just need to borrow him."

"Borrow?" Cassie frowned. Not another dating game. No more pop-ups. "Look, if this is another—"

"And his plane."

"His plane...?"

"Yes." Robyn took a deep breath. "I'm going after Alex."

"Alex? But why? I thought that was over."

Robyn gave her a vulnerable look. "I did, too. I tried, Cass, you know I did." She shrugged, looking conflicted. "But then I got an e-mail from a friend of his. An artist. He was mad at me."

"At you? But why?"

Robyn sighed a little shakily. "Because of Alex. He said Alex won't sculpt anymore. He doesn't want to."

Cassie rolled her eyes. "Great. Alex's Talent beckons again. Don't fall for it."

"No, Cass. It's not like that this time. It's not that he *can't* create. He just *won't*. He threw all his equipment into the Dumpster and then drove off to this remote cabin out by the lake. That was yesterday. This afternoon—if I don't get there in time—he's hopping on a plane to Mexico."

"I don't know, Robyn. This all just sounds like another Talent tantrum." Cassie was skeptical.

Robyn was not. "No. Alex did this because of me. Right after I sent him that e-mail telling him I was changing my e-mail address and I never wanted to hear from him or speak to him again. I guess that finally convinced Alex that I was serious about breaking it off with him. And he couldn't handle it. That's what his friend said.

"You know what this means? Alex gave up his art because he lost me. That makes me first. Do you see? I matter more to him than his art."

Cassie studied Robyn. "You really believe this?"

Robyn took a deep, shuddering breath and expelled it in a nervous whoosh. "Yeah. I do. He gets mad if he can't work, goes off to that old cabin to get away from me or whatever's bugging him. But he's never abandoned his art in favor of anything or anyone else. Never."

Robyn seemed certain and that glow in her eyes...Cassie wavered a little.

"One more thing, Cass. The more I think about it, the more I'm convinced that Alex and me meeting up out of the blue on the Internet...on a chat site with some fifty other people, choosing each other and making a connection...I don't think it was a coincidence. I think it was just meant to be. Fate."

Cassie felt the words like a blow straight to the gut.

"I want him back." Robyn raised her chin, looking strong and sure of herself. And Alex. That was new.

"Well. Fate plus real, physical evidence. What more do you want?" Cassie spoke quietly. "So, what do you need me to do?"

"Oh, thanks, Cass. I knew you'd help."

Cassie rolled her eyes. "Of course you did. If I didn't tar and feather you after the lesbian pretense, obviously I'm nuts enough to hang on to you no matter what."

Robyn laughed. "Good. Because I need you to sweet-talk Nick into flying me out to find Alex before he leaves for Mexico."

"Well, it just so happens I'm on my way to the airport right now."

SO IT WAS ONE of the longest car trips Cassie had ever taken, but not in physical distance. Robyn was convinced she was the new Dr. Phil, with scads of empowering advice for the lonely, the lovelorn and the stupid.

"...and this time I'm going to do things differently. I'm not living with him and I won't let him live off of me. He will have his own space and I will have mine and no way will I grow dependent on him again. I'm my own woman and I intend to stay that way. Any guy would *grovel* to have me...."

Cassie groaned. "Gag me."

"Huh?" Startled, Robyn glanced over.

Cassie pressed her lips together, fighting off a grin. "I just said 'gag me.' Hey, I'm thrilled you've come back into your own, but enough already. Lighten up. All these psychobabble 'affirmations' are making me nauseous."

With a mock growl, Robyn shoved Cassie.

"Hey, don't mess with the driver." But Cassie was grinning, so thrilled beyond words that healthy, happy Robyn was back. *Look out, Alex. You may not be ready for her.* She smiled at Robyn, who returned it, her eyes sparkling with humor and confidence. "Life is good."

Robyn nodded before pausing thoughtfully. "Could be better, though."

"Huh?" Cassie glanced at Robyn. "I thought we were deliriously happy just a moment ago. What could be broken already?"

"Well, I'm fixed. Alex *will* be fixed. What about you and Nick?"

"We...will be fixed, too. I have a plan. Sort of." She

glanced at Robyn. "Just let me do the talking first when we get to the airport. Okay?"

"Great idea. You soften him up, seduce him into taking me where I want to go, and then..." She shrugged, giving Cassie an evil smile. "At the next opportunity, you seduce him for yourself."

Cassie just laughed.

AFTER PARKING THE CAR and suggesting Robyn give her a few minutes before showing up, Cassie walked out to the private hangar and found Nick cursing over the engine of his Cessna.

"Of all the times to bomb on me, damn it. A few more minutes and I'd have been in the air and you'd likely have coughed and sputtered me into an early grave with Cas—"

"Nick?" Cassie's heart thudded unevenly. "Something...wrong with the plane?"

"Huh? Cassie! You came." Looking a little off-kilter, he stepped down from a low stool. Pivoting, he wiped his hands on a rag and slung it over the top of what looked to be a huge toolbox on wheels.

"Well...you asked me to. You said it was important. For the Web site, I mean."

He stopped in front of her and slid his hands backward into his hip pockets. "Yeah. The Web site. And other stuff, maybe."

"Other stuff?"

A shuffling sound had them both whirling to find Robyn hurrying in, her duffel bag slung over a shoulder. "Did he say it was okay?"

Cassie groaned. "You didn't give me half a chance to ask him, Robyn. It looks like his plane's on the blink anyway." Which was a relief and not. It was one more time that he didn't take off in the thing, but it also meant that the contraption could have failed and crashed on another flight. She couldn't deal. She couldn't deal. She couldn't deal.

Which meant no Nick.

Which meant...she couldn't deal, she couldn't deal, she couldn't deal. God, she was a mess. Maybe this was all a mistake. If she were this conflicted still...

"What's going on, Cassie?" Nick glanced between Cassie and Robyn, his gaze slanting downward to include Robyn's duffel bag.

"Well...we have a favor to ask of you."

"But I'll pay the fare or charter or whatever! I'm not begging for charity, just convenience—"

Cassie shot Robyn an impatient glance.

"Sorry." Robyn eased off.

Cassie turned back to Nick.

"Let me guess. She wants to fly somewhere and I'm the pilot?"

"Well...yeah. She needs to get to Alex. He's out at some remote cabin by the lake and she needs to find him before he flies to Mexico this afternoon."

Nick raised an eyebrow, his gaze still on Cassie. "Really. And Alex is the ex? From the breakup that's responsible for all the funky dating maneuvers?"

Robyn and Cassie winced.

"The reason you kept throwing Robyn at me when all I really wanted was a chance with you?"

The women winced again.

Nick dropped his voice. "And the reason you and I finally ran into each other again..."

Cassie stared, remembering. Becky's stupid party. The sports bar encounter and his help afterward. Dessert and laughs after the speed-dating bonanza. The lesbian fiasco...and their intimacy afterward. Her heart thumped. "Yeah."

Nick nodded slowly, his eyes on Cassie. "Okay. I'll do it."

"Just like that?" Robyn was amazed.

Cassie couldn't yet speak. Nick's gaze was still fixed on hers.

"Just like that." Nick murmured it.

"Then let's go." Robyn reached in and snagged Nick's arm. "Time's wasting and I'm withering."

As Robyn's words registered, Cassie glanced up. Her lips quirked. "Withers? What *withers?*"

Robyn grinned. "Nothing yet and I have no intention of finding out. But..." She raised an eyebrow at Nick, who looked less than enthused at the idea of leaving Cassie. "The sooner you dump me off at Alex's, the sooner you can come back here...."

Nick grinned. "Then let's go."

Cassie took a deep breath, nodding. "So, when can you get this thing up in the air?" Nick was a professional. He knew what he was doing. He'd have the Cessna in working condition in no time and they could all get Robyn to Alex and then back again. It would be okay. Cassie had flown in it before, so that was no big deal and—

"Cessna's not going anywhere today." Nick grimaced. "We'll have to take the Piper." He gave Cassie an apologetic glance. "And it's a two-seater, so..."

Cassie's breath hitched. "So you two fly and...I wait here?"

He nodded.

Gee, there was cause for a few worst-case scenarios. Her best friend and the man she loved, alone on a plane. A tiny little plane, way, way up in the big blue sky, far above the rocky ground below... One little mechanical glitch and *kablooey*, there went life as Cassie knew it.

A nice storm could blow up out of nowhere and *blam* goes the plane into the side of a hill. Ozarks weren't really mountains, so you couldn't say it would crash into a mountain—which sounded sufficiently dramatic and horrific—but *blam* was *blam*. Cassie wasn't fond of *blam* when it meant Nick's plane, plus Nick and Robyn, smashing into something hard and unforgiving.

"Cass." Nick spoke patiently, his voice low and understanding. But commanding. He'd obviously tried to get her attention a few times, but she'd gotten lost in her mental blatherings. "Cass?"

"Mmm?" It was the most she could manage without revealing her discordant thoughts.

"Have a little faith. Okay?"

The man saw right through her. It was completely unnerving. She watched as he retrieved something bulky from the Cessna and carted it over to the Piper. He checked the plane over and made a couple of calls while Robyn stowed her duffel and paced the hangar.

When Nick strode back to Cassie, his eyes dark and

thoughtful as they met hers, Cassie tried to settle her nerves. Small talk, maybe. "So, um. Where are Chad and Jerry?"

"Chad's out of town today, won't be back for another few days. Jerry's got business meetings and I don't expect to see him until late tomorrow." Nick gazed down at her, his lips spreading in a wicked, coaxing grin. "Why? Afraid you'll have to call them to rescue my broken, dead body from my broken, dead plane?"

"Nick!" Cassie glared at him, but his teasing loosened the knots in her belly.

He rolled his eyes, though his smile said he understood. "Take it easy. Think about stats class. I'm a damn good pilot. Remember?"

She hesitated, then nodded. A firm nod.

"Good girl." He kissed her hard, then called Robyn to follow him.

As Cassie watched, with rounded eyes, Nick pushed the plane out of the hangar and soon he and Robyn were inside, waving as he taxied toward the runway. *Too soon, too soon.* She wanted nothing more than to call them back—

She groaned, low and long. Totally disgusted with herself. "God, get a life, Cassie. When did you become a fearful old priss?" She was sick of her own thoughts. Still, she watched until the plane was safely in the air and growing smaller with distance.

"Well. They're up. So, I guess I could..." She looked around. "Wait around here? I'd go nuts." She frowned, her earlier idea gelling into bigger possibilities. "Or...I could take a leap of faith. It could require preparation, however." She smiled thoughtfully.

Purposeful now, she ran to her car and drove back to her apartment, where she dug through boxes for her Christmas decorations. She really, really had a thing for Christmas lights. And so she had many...

After stowing everything in her car, she took a quick shower, glanced frantically at the clock and ran out the door. She'd have about forty-five minutes, give or take, so she'd better get a move on.

Back at the airport again, she lugged the big tote she'd packed out of her trunk and carried it to the hangar. Luckily, she'd left after Nick and Robyn had, so the door was still unlocked. Dropping the tote on a workbench, she got busy.

Several minutes and a quandary or two later, she stood back, a little breathless now, with a blanket in her arms to take in the full picture. She'd tangled extension cords and fairy lights wherever practicable in the hangar—along workbenches, draped over fixtures or hardware, even, with effort, around the cockpit of the ailing Cessna.

She knew from experience that, after landing, Nick would stop the plane outside the hangar and shut off the engine. It would have to be physically pushed backward into the building. Of course, she intended to distract him well before he was able to do any such thing.

Just as she pondered yet again whether she dared to just lay the blanket where she wanted, she heard the roar of an incoming plane. The airport was small enough that the planes weren't coming right on top of each other, so an individual plane...she squinted into the sky...could mean Nick was back. The timing was right.

Cassie walked toward the still-open hangar door, fully intending to close the thing to ensure her surprise, when she got a closer look at the incoming plane. And the banner it towed right behind it.

*Nick loves Cassie.*

The plane circled the airport, once, twice, three times and she heard cheers echoing from other hangars, even as she felt tears running down her cheeks.

*Nick loves Cassie.*

Her knees weakened and she leaned against the door opening, watching as the plane circled yet one more time before departing slightly and turning to prepare for landing. It came closer and closer and Cassie felt her heart pumping harder and faster, as though it might burst before she could even jump the guy in return.

Oh, God, but she loved him. Sign, indeed. She choked on a laugh before hurrying back into the hangar. She plugged in the fairy lights and flipped off all other lights. It saved her from having to watch the landing, which could only be excruciating, even if she knew Nick was competent and experienced.

He was right. She could grow more and more confident in his abilities. It had already begun. She didn't even feel like throwing up at the idea of him landing the tinier of his two planes.

The growing roar warned her and she hurriedly closed the hangar door to preserve her surprise. The sound grew louder and closer until, with a deafening change in tone, it shut off.

In the ensuing silence, Cassie swore she could hear her heart beating. Then she heard a distinctive clang of the hangar door rolling up. The dimming light of dusk seeped into the wonderland she had created. She waited breathlessly.

After a few moments of surprised silence, Nick took a few steps inside. He gazed around himself before letting his eyes land on Cassie. She fidgeted slightly, so nervous and yet not, and cuddled the blanket closer. Blanket. She still hadn't put the blanket anywhere, couldn't dump it, didn't know—

"Cass."

She inhaled, let it out shakily. "Hi. You're back."

"Yeah. Did you...see?"

She pressed a hand to her lips and nodded, tears welling all over again.

*Nick loves Cassie.*

He moved closer. "Well...you said you needed a sign to help you make your decision about us." He glanced over his shoulder at the plane he'd just landed, before turning back to her with a boyish grin. "That was the best I could do." His eyes were bright with hope.

She gave a watery chuckle. "Yeah, I did say that, didn't I? Leave it to a man to take it literally."

"But it's true, Cassie, and it means everything in the world to me. I was hoping it would mean something to you, too. I do love you and I wanted you and the whole world to know it. No doubts. No questions."

Cassie choked on a laugh, her emotions too big to contain. "Well...that ought to do it."

"And that disk I sent you...well, it's a mock-up picture of what I just did, banner and all. Jerry doctored it for me because I didn't want him here for the real deal, but I want it up there. On the Web site. It's, technically, a demo for aerial advertising, one of the services we offer. But it also gives me a way to broadcast the truth to the world."

"Oh, Nick." With a running leap, she landed in his arms. "God, but I love you, too. I tried not to. A long time ago and then again in the past few weeks. It's no use. I'm hooked." She giggled unsteadily. "And I love your sign."

"I hoped you would." He held her fast. "I wanted you here to see and hear the real thing first. Nick loves Cassie. In fact, he adores her. From her quirky fatalism that's really just a romantic streak that's *way* up there on the fairy-tale scale...." He squeezed her and continued above her embarrassed mutterings "...to her smart mouth, to her beautiful smile, to her caring heart. I love you, Cassandra Smythe."

She gave a watery chuckle. "Then shut up and kiss me."

He did so and she responded with enough fervor to have him staggering backward. She giggled and then squealed when he pretended to drop her. The blanket fluttered but didn't fall.

"Hey, what's this?" He gave her a teasing look as he tugged on the blanket now nearly draped around both of them. "Were you cold?"

She smiled, slow and teasing. "Not quite. In fact, I was getting a little warm just thinking about it. And you and me."

"Really."

"Mmm, hmm. Everything's backward, though. The idea was to drape *ourselves* over the blanket."

His eyes narrowed and darkened over a devilish grin. "I like that idea."

She blinked in mock helplessness. "But I just couldn't find a single place to put it. The floor's kind of hard." She wrinkled her nose. "And a little dirty. You have a desk, but there's a computer sitting on it. And all your workbenches seem occupied or too small. Why, every spare surface seems to be covered with all kinds of important stuff. And your apartment's so far away. I just don't know what to do." She blinked innocently, very much the damsel in certain distress.

He gave her a knowing look. "Then, allow me." He planted a hard kiss on her mouth before sliding her arms from around his neck, then carried the blanket to the Cessna.

Cassie stared, then giggled as she watched him open the door and wrestle the front seat forward. "But, Nick. Think of the trauma. We're molesting your *plane.*"

After flipping the blanket open over the back seat, Nick turned back to face her with a grin. "I think of it more as baptizing it."

"Gosh, Nick." She laughed. "That's downright open-minded of you."

He shrugged modestly and held out a hand. "My lady? Your cockpit awaits."

She laughed helplessly but took his hand. "You're shameless."

"I know. Just remember that I'm the pilot, baby."

"Come fly the friendly skies?"

He growled and tugged her off her feet and into his arms. Somehow, some way, they ended up in the tiny back seat.

"You know, if I weren't so hot for your amazing body, I could make you cringe over this." She started tugging on his shirt, thinking the Drummonds, as kinky as they were, certainly had an excellent idea.

"I know." He gasped when she raked a fingernail over his nipple and tugged the shirt over his head. "Have mercy."

She showed none, just attached her lips to his and rocked his world by pouring every ounce of feeling into her kiss. He growled low into her throat and returned the kiss with fervor, his body hardening and moving purposely against hers.

She inhaled sharply. "How?"

He gave a rough laugh. "You'll see. Ever do it in a car?"

Her laughter broke off on a gasp and a sigh as he tugged her tank top off and took unfair advantage of her braless state. Pausing, breathing heavily, he glanced up at her, a gleam in his eyes.

The pause steadied her. Briefly. She had unfinished business. "Um, Nick?"

He nuzzled her cleavage, rubbing a cheek against each breast, his eyes closed. Her words finally registered. Well, the fact that she'd spoken did, but the words... "Hmm?"

"Count pigeons."

"What?" Pigeons...didn't register. No, he was still too enthralled, now with the curve of her waist, that little dip right there. Amazing. Seemed to defy logic and gravity and every bit of self-control a man might have at his disposal.

"Pigeons. *Count pigeons.*"

At last her words registered and he started laughing, still nuzzling at a dainty rib.

"Hey, that tickles. Quit!" She squealed, squirming and giggling.

"Count pigeons, huh?"

"Well, I'm just trying to be helpful. We had sort of...a delicate situation before."

"Delicate? I'll show you delicate." Growling, he dipped his head to her breasts, hearing her gasp. Smiling craftily against one, he began. Slow, methodical torture. Soon he had her panting, then mewling, then crooning, perhaps even—dare he say it?—emitting a high-pitched guttural, almost warbling....

"Oh. My." She breathed the words a few moments later, awe drenching every syllable. "I don't yodel, Nick."

"Are you sure? Because it really sounds like you do."

"You made me— I just— And you haven't even—"

He smiled, slow. "No, but I will."

Her eyes widened and she gave him a breathless look. "Yeah?"

"Oh, yeah." Off went the shorts. And with them, a

sweet lacy number that might pass for panties. It seemed a shame not to admire them on her at his leisure, but they were pressed for space and he damn well might need to count some of those pigeons soon. He'd only made her come once and he'd vowed to himself...

"Nick." She dragged his mouth to hers and shoved him backward so he slumped into a half-seated position. He'd sit completely upright if he could, but he'd bust Nick Junior if he did.

Not that Junior minded anything at all, now that Cassie had climbed on top.

"Hold on, Nick." She popped the button on his fly. "We're going for a little ride now." *Zzip.*

"I thought I was the pilot."

She smiled evilly. "Consider yourself hijacked." Carefully she tugged the waistband of his shorts out of the way and—

"Mercy." He gasped when her hands found purchase and did something amazing—

"Teach you to make me yodel in a public place." She shifted. Just so.

He eyed her, his brain fogging. "I thought you liked it."

"Mmm. I did." She deftly rolled a condom on—the woman was resourceful—and then rose up carefully, purposefully, her eyes hot and fixed on his. "So will you."

She lowered herself, smooth as silk, and took him deep. He growled low. "Pigeons. One...two..."

She laughed breathlessly, shaking his control a little

more when all her muscles seemed to quiver in tandem and even counterpoint.

When he gasped again, she began to move on him. "Do you yodel, too, Nick?"

Her giggling taunt grounded his control. He was not done yet. Giving her a rakish grin, he grasped her hips, tilting her just so...then he thrust deep and rhythmically, the friction hitting her just where it should.

"Nick!" came out as a squeak and she caught her breath as she came, helplessly, her body convulsing over his.

"Oh, yeah." Holding her body in place, he continued to thrust, slow and evenly until she recovered.

Carefully, as though emerging through a fog, Cassie gazed at Nick, his face shining with sweat and lust and love. The man was a marvel. "You. You are a fraud."

He tipped his hips, eliciting another gasp and shudder from her. "Yeah?"

"You come on as the poor, misunderstood—stud who's not really a stud— But you—"

He grinned, hands sliding off her hips and veering toward more intimate territory. She couldn't believe he hadn't even touched her south of the border yet. Unbelievable. But now he was going to—

"You earned that reputation." She forced the words out.

"Mmm. The hard way." The border was breached and she saw a fourth, even a fifth orgasm before Nick stopped counting pigeons. He groaned as he thrust deep and let himself go.

Feeling as weak as gelatin, and almost as smart, Cassie collapsed on his chest. Her heart still raced along like a giddy little pony who'd found her stud for life. Cassie knew exactly how the pony felt. "I love you, Nick. And not just because you are Super Stallion in bed. Cowboy, hell. Somebody's maligned your reputation. Stallion. Pure stallion. But I'd love you even if you were a pretend cowboy."

Chuckling, he cupped her face in his hands and met her eyes, his own glowing and dark. "I love you, too. And, for the record, nothing short of a stallion could keep up with something as hot as you."

She rewarded his blatant flattery with a deep, soulful kiss that had him twitching to life again. She giggled against his lips.

He smiled back.

She sighed. "I just can't believe... Nick I wish everyone were as happy as this. Everyone should be."

He nibbled on her lip. "Would you settle for Robyn being happy?"

"Hmm?"

"Alex met her at the plane. The man looked like he'd lived—only barely—through a world-class catastrophe. And he greeted Robyn at the plane like she was the Red Cross."

Cassie pulled back, wide-eyed. "Really?"

"Really. Turns out some mutual friend gave Alex the heads-up and he knew to look for her. I imagine they're probably doing what we're doing now. Satisfied?"

Her heart swelling with feeling, she managed a grin. "Satisfied? Me? Oh, not just yet."

Eyelids drooping in sexy interest, he tugged her close. "Tell me more."

She pulled back to give him a frown of mock concern. "Well, only if you feel...*capable*..."

He gave her a stern look. "Obviously, I have some damage control still ahead of me. I have a reputation to consider here."

"Reputation? Oh, no. Not after towing that banner behind you across the sky, you don't." She gave him a provoking look, her lips curving and her heart full with the knowledge of exactly what that message had meant to both of them. Of course, the heat in her cheeks was nothing less than one hundred percent turned-on woman.

He grinned. "I'm working on a different reputation now."

"Oh, yeah?" She gave him a suspicious look. "And what might that be, Cowboy?"

"That I'm a one-woman flyboy. Yours."

"Hey, I like that. It sounds mysterious. Empowering even. You know, like I conquered an urban legend or something."

With a look promising retribution, he leaned in for a gnawing kiss to her throat. His chest rumbled low, part hungry growl, part purr of satisfaction.

She gasped as a thousand nerve endings pinged simultaneously and her heart soared wild and free. She hauled him to her lips for a deeper kiss, feeling his heart thump loudly against hers and his arms tighten around her.

Destiny, luck, free will...it didn't matter who did the choosing. Nick was all hers. There was no escaping that reality, and who the hell would want to, anyway? She was keeping.

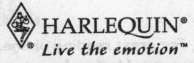

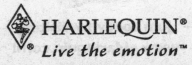

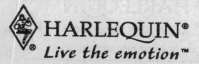